The Nectar Called Grace

S Pavithra Ram

Thirukudanthai

"Where a rich garden of honey-fed flowers perennially grows,
Where dense creepers, paddy fields and groves abound,
Where the river Ponni (Cauvery) flows in abundance,
Carrying with it the choicest gems and riches to the land.
In that town where the learned dwell,
Where flags atop the mansions fly high up, unto the sky, gently stroking the moon;
In this land of bountiful wealth- the Thirukudanthai,
Rested on the celestial serpent- the Adisesha;
And worshipped by the chants of Vedic scholars,
Oh, Supreme Lord of the Universe!
I surrender at your feet,
In prayer to remove all the hurdles that come my way."

These words, in the translation of a *pasuram*, a Tamil hymn by Saint *Thirumangai Azhwar*, capture the beauty, bounty and greatness of the blessed town of *Thirukudanthai.*

On a drive down the highway leading to the city of *Kumbakonam*, also known as *Kudanthai*, in South India, the flourish, flora and sprawling fields of paddy stretched on either side of the road as far as eyes could reach, stand true to the timeless words of the *Azhwar*, to this day.

Nestled in the heart of the temple town of Kumbakonam lies a magnificent temple of Lord Vishnu.

Prominent among the venerated 108 *divyadesams, Thirukudanthai,* as it is referred to in the hymns of the *Azhwars*, is said to be the birthplace of Goddess *Mahalakshmi,* as Goddess *Komalavalli.*

Lord Vishnu, as Lord Aravamudan, descended in his celestial chariot to seek her hand in marriage.

Known for its architectural splendour, the temple with its mighty *Rajagopuram*, expansive courtyards, and the sanctum in the design of a massive chariot drawn by elephants and horses, called the *Vaideeka Vimana*, transcendental in its form and grandeur, the intricate sculptural work all around, their mere sight and ambience could leave one in a divine stupor.

"*Aravamudan*" in Tamil means a nectar of insatiable sweetness!

Captivating as the name is the presence of the presiding deity, Lord Aravamudan, an embodiment of compassion and grace, tranquillising the hearts of devotees with his quintessential sweetness and endearing smile. Fondly referred to as Lord Amudan, the Lord in his majestic form reclined on the celestial serpent, the *Adisesha,* and in the form of the festival deity, Lord Sarangapani, gallantly holding "sarangam", the bow, along with his consort, Goddess Komalavalli, stand to this day as refuge to the thousands of devotees who throng the temple round the year.

By their boundless compassion and love, the Lord and the Goddess, heal, nurture, protect, and bestow boons to their devotees, near and far.

The chime of the temple bells, the distant chant of the hymns, the sight of the *Raja Gopuram*, the gentle breeze carrying the scent of the holy *Porthamarai* pond, the peace and serenity they all carry are the precious luxuries of each one living within the precincts of the streets surrounding the temple.

Their lives and livelihoods are intricately connected to the temple, in one way or the other.

It was one of the festival days at the temple. The streets were being cleared off the vehicles, to make way for the procession of the festival deity that was to begin shortly. Ladies clad in traditional attire were competing with each other, drawing large *Kolams* in front of their houses, to welcome the Lord with his consorts on a palanquin. The flower vendors made a booty on these days, with swarms of people thronging from all over the country. A field day for hawkers selling quaint knick-knacks, catching the attention of every child in the crowd.

With the sun finally taking shelter behind the clouds, after a long day's labour, it was a breezy evening in the Tamil month of *Chithirai*, spanning from mid-April to mid-May. A group of boys playing around the temple entrance, frenzied by the festive vibe, watching the lights, decorations and all the action at the temple.

A little one among them stood at the entrance, crooning his neck all the way up, gaping at the towering temple *Gopuram* that seemed to emerge from the sky, the dense cloud looming over it and strings of colourful lights hanging from top glittering like stars.

He was disturbed by a loud honk as an imposing full-size SUV was brought to a halt before the entrance. He watched a couple of men alight from the vehicle and women, draped in silk and riches, step out from the back seats.

There was something strange about their demeanour that he couldn't quite relate to.

The younger of the men asked one of the volunteers outside the temple, "Do you know where we can find Kumaran? We had spoken to him to organize our *darshan* today."

"We are unable to reach him over the phone. Minister Sir and his family have to leave for a meeting," He added in a hushed tone, pointing to the senior man beside him.

"He will be inside the temple, Sir," replied the volunteer and sent one of his teammates to look for Kumaran.

The family followed the volunteer inside the temple. People were lined up in a long queue to have the *darshan* of the presiding deity.

There was a group of men and women decorating the inner courtyard of the temple with flowers and *Kolams* all along the pathway where the Lord would be carried through, in a palanquin.

The volunteer returned, stating that Kumaran was not at the temple and that he was expected to be there at any moment. The senior man, introduced as a Minister, began to make a scene, stating that he was getting delayed for a meeting and demanding to meet the temple officials.

Komalavalli, the daughter of the head priest, was engrossed in drawing a grand, intricate *Kolam* design at the centre of the pathway, singing to herself a Tamil hymn. Disturbed by the commotion around, Komala slowly lifted her head and looked towards them.

"Manikanda, what is the matter?" she asked the volunteer. The volunteer ran up to her and explained the situation.

Sizing up the family from far, the airs and the pomp, she said to Manikandan, "Why don't you call Amudan? He must be in the *vahana mandapam*."

Manikandan stood with a dubious look at her, more troubled by her proposition. She was amused by her own suggestion, in fact, as one could tell from the smile she stifled. With a reassuring nod at Manikandan, she coaxed him onto the mission, eager to watch what was to ensue.

Within minutes, they could hear the roar and rumble from afar. The people in the queue, the volunteers around the temple and the ladies drawing *Kolams* all waited, with bated breath as a tall man in his early twenties, leapt out of the *vahana mandapam*, clad in a dhoti folded up to his knees and the *angavasthram* wrapped around his forehead, and charged towards them in the gait of a wild elephant, the *Thiruman Sricharanam* on his forehead glittering brighter through the beads of his sweat. His eyes, like two balls of fire, turned to the man he was introduced to and held his gaze. Amudan needed no introduction to most others in the temple watching on.

Shaken by his sheer appearance, the Minister's aide slowly gathered himself and said, "We spoke to Kumaran on our way. He had promised to arrange the *darshan* of the deity today. Minister Sir is already late for a party meeting!"

When Amudan cut in, saying, "Now, what should I do? If you want to meet Kumaran, you can wait here till he comes. If you want to have *Perumal*'s *darshan* you can join the queue over there. *Darshan* will take a long time. You can see the crowd!" He reasoned.

As the man interrupted him, prompting that the Minister was getting delayed, Amudan brusquely said, "Then you will have to come another day. When you can wait!" He added with an admonitory pause, holding the gaze of the Minister again.

Loud as a thousand stones left rolling at a time, his words, like swords, went slicing through. The Minister was left shocked and fuming!

Turning to the volunteer, Amudan hurled, "Why are you staring at me now? Have you cleared the vehicles? On all the roads? Have they checked the power backup? Is the work on the chariot done? You were supposed to oversee that!" He bawled and the volunteer meekly whizzed away like the wind.

While the Minister censured his man, saying, "Can't you arrange even this simple thing? Do I have to deal with all 'these'?"

Shooting a threatening glance at Amudan, the Minister led his wife and daughter outside the temple. Amudan, without a moment's delay, sprinted back to the *Vahana Mandapam* to join the other volunteers preparing the *vahana* for the evening's procession.

"Why did you have to call *Anna*? You know he cannot entertain this," asked Bhooma, Amudan's younger sister.

"Oh, that is exactly why I called your *Anna*, my dear," replied Komala with a chuckle.

"The only times when I find his perpetual frown and boiling temper to be of any use!" she commented." Don't you agree? Who else can bring down all their heaps of pride and affluence to dust in a moment?" she said while adding the finishing touches to the *kolam*.

" Well, you surely got him in trouble, now, "muttered Bhooma sullenly.

"As if he does not get into trouble otherwise! The other day he violently grabbed the phone from a girl trying to take a picture of Lord Sarangapani during *thirumanjanam*. The poor one wailed in shock and your brother was close to being roughed up by the girl's father. Kumaran came to his rescue as always," she said, shaking her head hopelessly.

Bhooma left with no words for defence, dropped her head down. Just then they heard Kumaran's voice as he scurried in with the Minister's family, profusely apologising to the senior man.

With a swift glance at Bhooma, and a gesture of his hand, gathering where Amudan was, he rushed the family down the VIP gate for the *darshan*.

"There, again he comes to the rescue!" muttered Komala, watching Bhooma grinning with relief.

Just as Kumaran walked the family out after the *darshan,* they shuddered as they saw Amudan standing across, supervising a team of volunteers finishing the flower decorations.

His steely eyes took on Kumaran as they all walked past him. He never cared to spare the others a glance.

"Amuda, I will be back," uttered Kumaran, and led the family out of the temple.

A practice Amudan could never digest, much less entertain!

"Your friend, Amudan, embarrassed us a lot. He did not know whom he was dealing with," recounted the Minister with a condescending smile.

"He means no offence, Sir. He has been serving at the temple even as a little boy. To him, *Perumal* and the temple are bigger than everything else! We are all here for his assistance. He is like a child, though! Never holds anything against anyone. Please don't take his words to heart," replied Kumaran, as he opened the vehicle door for the Minister.

"Of course, a child! Too small for me," mumbled the Minister with a chortle. "He has to grow up, son! He has to be careful" softly threatened the Minister as he handed a cheque of donation to the temple.

"Thank you, Sir," said Kumaran with a courteous smile and added, "*Perumal* is there to protect our Amudan."

"Yes! Yes!" replied the gentleman with a smirk." I see you have a lot of respect for your friend. Take care of him."

"I will, Sir. He is like my brother. I will do anything for him," he said with folded hands. The car slowly moved past him.

It was soon time for the festivities to begin. The conch was blown and the *Mangala Aarthi* was offered to the deities seated majestically on the Elephant *vahana*, ready to be lifted by a gallant group of men volunteers, who prided in calling themselves *Sripadamthangis*- the bearers of the Lord's palanquín!

"*Hecharika*!" commanded Amudan, standing in front, as he, along with the entire squad of the *Sripadamthangis*, lifted and hoisted the giant *vahana* on their shoulders in a sweep of a sequential motion. A moment of spectacle, it will remain, any number of times you may have witnessed it!

A group of Vedic scholars, clothed in a traditional attire wearing the 12 *Thiruman Sricharanam* on them, well versed in the Vedas and the Tamil hymns of the Azhwars referred to as the "*Tamizh Vedam* or the *Naalaayira Divya Prabhandam*" lined up before the deities.

They recited in unison the verses from the *Divya Prabhandham,* their voices in sync, in a tune that has been taught and passed on over many generations now. The roaring chants of the *Divya prabhandham* and the Vedas, with Lord Sarangapani and his consorts seated on the *vahana* for all of them to see; those moments of sublime divinity held every eye that stood witness, a captive.

Once the *Shatari*, bearing the holy feet of the Lord was placed on their heads, the *Prabhandha Goshti,* as they were called, led the procession and the *Veda Parayana Goshti* followed the Lord in the procession.

Amudan on one side, and Kumaran on the other, holding the ends of poles of the *vahana* resting on their shoulders, lead the rest of the *Sripadamthangis* on their march ahead. Like a trained battalion of soldiers, their synchronized movement was quite a visual treat.

Differences

Komala was the only child of Narayana *Bhattar* and Ranganayaki. To the people of the *Agraharam*, she epitomized the goddess of knowledge. Komala, with her exemplary scholastic achievements in school and college, was the pride of the town and a favourite student of Amudan's father, Ramanujam. Komala now taught at the town school and also taught the children and women of the locality, the Tamil hymns of the *Azhwars*, with utmost passion. To her, the hymns of the *Azhwars*, rich in moral values and life lessons, were not a mere religious text but meant to be an essential part of the curriculum for young minds, to mould them into strong-willed, virtuous, and erudite adults. Her vision to deliver a wholesome education made her more conscientious in her role as a teacher, setting even higher moral standards for herself.

She strung garlands for Lord *Aravamudan* every day and drew the most exquisite *kolams* in the temple, hoping each day that the Lord would notice it and would be reminded of her. She believed Lord Amudan to be her bosom friend. Whether she was happy, angry, or sad, she was always in a conversation with Him.

There were a few others like her, throbbing with aspirations and eyes full of vision. They all grew up together in this small town.

Kumaran, his family owned a rice mill in the town that employed most of the local people for generations. Kumaran's business was his mainstay, but his vital interest lay in the well-being of the town.

His constant strive and pride rested on bringing to the town the best of facilities and infrastructure. His curious mind looked for a business idea all around him, saw every new person he met as a potential resource, and never shirked investing in them both. Amudan was indeed a mission beyond all that- the mission to protect, provide for and always stand by Amudan. Come what may!

Their friendship was quite a wonder to the people of the town! They belonged to different communities, and different family backgrounds and were distinctly different in their natures and the bond they shared was on a different plain as well, pristine and unyielding to societal norms.

Desikan was another friend of Amudan, the only son of a Vedic scholar serving at the temple. For Desikan, his urge always lay on exploring the world beyond, as if something were kept from him on purpose and which he was determined to pursue. He felt trapped within the precincts of the tradition, culture and mindset of his immediate surroundings and felt an overpowering ache to break free from it in every way he could.

Kumaran and Desikan, though, had one thing in common- Amudan, their grounding factor. Although Amudan was never too vocal or vociferous about his opinions, his validation was very crucial for both, whether they sought it or fought it.

They both were indeed more educationally qualified, yet Amudan's sharp native sense, and his very earthy, clear, and intuitive thought process, always amazed them.

Even after Desikan moved out of the *Agraharam* to pursue a career in law, he looked forward to the long phone conversations with Amudan when he would rant over a political situation or an instance of social injustice that he was struggling to gulp in. He looked up to Amudan's rational take on every little thing, his ability to quash a long line of argument with an innocent "Why?" Or "How?" candidly driving home a whole new perspective. Desikan was often left wondering as to what lay within the humble, simpleton persona that Amudan carried!

Kumaran and Desikan, though worlds apart in their thoughts and ways, Amudan remained their focal point, a cause dearer than their lives that they would fight the world for!

If there was a person Amudan cared for more than anyone else, it was his friend, Govindan, who served at the temple as a priest. A Vedic scholar and an ardent devotee of Lord Rama. Having lost his parents at a very young age, Govindan treated Lord Sarangapani and Goddess Komalavalli as his parents. Known for his prowess in the Vedas and the Hindu scriptures, he was considered a gifted child and much respected by the people of the *Agraharam*.

The temple was where Govindan spent most of his time, immersed in the reading of *Srimad Ramayana* and in service to the Lord and Goddess. He didn't know much of the world beyond that. A couple of years younger than himself, Amudan cared for Govindan as his younger brother and guarded him as much as he guarded the deities in the temple.

"Come, Amuda! *Akka* and *Athimber* are waiting to have lunch with you," welcomed Perundevi, Amudan's mother, as the latter walked into their house.

"When did you all come?" enquired Amudan, courteously smiling at Ranganathan, his brother-in-law.

"We came a couple of hours ago. Was wondering if we should come to the temple to see you before we left. Then, *Appa* told us that once the temple closes in the noon, you will come home anyway," remarked Padma, his elder sister.

Amudan quietly joined them for lunch.

"Your bank manager reference for my friend worked wonders, Amuda. The loan process was so quick. He got the funds on time. I hope he thanked you enough," remarked Ranganathan.

"Of course!" replied Amudan.

After the first course was served, Padma, unable to hold her tongue any longer, uttered," Amuda, have you thought about what *Athimber* had asked you last time? Will you be interested in joining his business? He always keeps saying, "*If only Amudan joined us, it would be of great help!*"

Amudan awkwardly looked up while his brother-in-law pitched in, saying, "Will you not let him eat in peace? Where is the hurry, Padma?" he chided.

" Oh! Please don't say that to him. He is already too laid back on these things. All his friends have moved out of the country and settled in good jobs. Left to him, Amudan would spend the rest of his life at the temple," she said with a smirk.

Amudan continued to eat, not looking up from his plate.

"Ranga, I am so relieved that you care for Amudan and Bhooma as your own siblings. What more can we ask? They must be very lucky," commented Ramanujam, Amudan's father.

"Oh, don't worry at all, *Appa*. He was in fact suggesting an alliance for our Bhooma last week. Let's see!" gloated Padma.

Amudan sneaked a glance at Bhooma who was coldly staring back at him.

"You can trust your son-in-law to conduct a grand wedding for your second daughter as well," added Padma with a wink at her little sister.

" I know. I am happy she has at least one brother to worry about her and her welfare. Not everyone can think beyond themselves and work for the welfare of their family. It is very rare. At least for us," remarked Ramanujam, never missing a chance to taunt his son.

"Why do you talk like that, *Appa*? *Anna* knows what he has to do for me and when. We don't have to tell him. He is the one who will get me married and no one else!" sputtered Bhooma.

"Bhooma, quiet!" snapped Amudan, taken aback by her tone and words.

"Why do you quieten her, Amuda? She is only covering up for you. That's how sisters are! We can never let you down, even if you don't care for us. At least don't shout! You are getting more and more short-tempered these days, Amuda. Watch out! That is why I think a change of place should help you," Padma retorted.

Ranganathan and Perundevi were mute audiences to the fiery exchanges.

"Amuda, what do you have to say to that?" Padma asked again.

"What is there to say? You answer most of your questions about me, anyway," he muttered without looking up.

"Will you move to Chennai to join Athimber's business?" she asked

"No," he replied, looking right into her eyes.

"See how curtly he responds, *Appa*!" she complained, her eyes welling up now.

"How long can you live like this, Amuda? You will need us one day. You cannot be so self-centred! All the time, doing what pleases you. You have to act more responsibly."

"We will take care of *Appa, Amma* and Bhooma. At least think about your future! You cannot wither away your life in this town!" reproached Padma.

"Forget it, Padma. Don't waste your energy! He is very stubborn. More than you can imagine. There is no use talking to him. I have given up on him long back. I am happy you have settled well and if we manage to get Bhooma married as well, I will consider all my duties done," said Ramanujam, darting a glance at his wife.

"We are all worrying so much for you. You don't care about anything, is it? Does it not affect you one bit that *Appa* feels this way?" asked Padma.

Amudan merely stared at her.

"Say something! We are not talking to the wall," she yelled.

"What can I say? If talking about me this way makes you all feel better, so be it!" he replied.

"What are you talking? If you can't understand that we are all talking for your good, no one can help you!" she remarked.

"All right! *Akka*, when I need help, I will ask you. For now, you have done enough. I have had a stomach full," he mumbled as he rose.

" I will shut up, Amuda. Please stay. I come here all the way to spend a few hours with my family, can't you bear with me for even that short a while? You never come to see me. You never call or respond. I know you have no affection for me..." she choked out and began to cry.

"That is it! This is how it always ends," roared Amudan, and stormed out of the room.

Minutes later, Ranganathan followed Amudan to his bicycle when Amudan, with a conciliatory smile, said, "Sorry, *Athimber*. I spoilt the family lunch. About your offer, I hope you don't mistake me." He candidly apologised.

"Of course! Don't mistake your sister as well. Although she is in Chennai, her mind is right here always.

Everything that catches her attention, be it a nice T-shirt, a fancy car or just a new dish that she tasted, she instantly thinks of you, "*If only our Amudan was here...*" she would go. Visit us, now and then. That will do. The more she sees you, the less she will worry," he pacified, as Amudan faintly nodded.

"By the way, Amuda, you should hear what Sarangan said to your father today," went on Ranganathan, referring to his son, Sarangan. "He has been totally enamoured by the miniature sculpture of Lord Aravamudan you had made for him. He carries it to school every day. Today when your father asked him what he wanted to become when he grew up, do you know what Sarangan replied? He said, *'I want to become a sculptor like Mama!'*"

Amudan burst into a chuckle at that.

What shock and dismay it was to Ramanujam to know that his grandson aspires for and treasures something that he had bundled up and cast away in the attic, as just another injudicious preoccupation of his son!

Sketches, paintings, and stone sculptures, of different sizes, from the tiniest piece of paper to wall-size cutouts or sculptures, everything carried just one image! Lord *Aravamudan* reclined on the *Adisesha*. What was most special about Amudan's works was how every minute feature, the expression, and the smile of the Lord, was perfectly captured in every piece, however big or small, like it was traced out of the original form.

Perundevi often recalled the words of the sculptor who had taught Amudan. "Sthapathi Thatha" as Amudan would call him, a very senior man, and an exponent in the craft, once said to Perundevi, " *He came here to learn from me. I taught him everything I knew. Today, he uses the same technique and materials, but his sculptures are not like any of ours. Can you see?*" the old man had said, pointing to the hundreds of sculptures piled along in his workshop.

"*I found his trick, finally,*" he revealed, sporting a naughty toothless grin.

"*We all try and create the image of Gods and Goddesses using our skill while your son brings to life his Perumal hidden inside every stone or paper. He never fails to find Him. That is the difference!*" he had remarked.

Cane and comfort

"Amuda! Amuda!" a voice roared across the walls of the temple.

Amudan rushed out of the sanctum in rage.

"*Enna da*? What do you want?" scowled Amudan.

"You have to leave. It is already late. Come along! I will drive you to Chennai," prodded Amudan's friend Desikan.

"I am not coming anywhere, Desika. I am not to taking up the job. I even informed the Secretary last night when she called. Now go back home and sleep. Get out!" ordered Amudan, pushing his friend by his shoulder.

Just as they were talking, Amudan's father, Ramanujam, walked in asking, "What is he saying, Desika? Is he ready to leave?"

In a softer voice, Amudan said, "*Appa*, I am not taking up the job. I am not going anywhere."

"You fool! You come with me," shouted Desikan, dragging Amudan out of the temple.

"Don't do this, Amuda. This is a great opportunity. Don't miss it. The only chance you have for a decent job! We cannot sit and watch you rot in this town and ruin your life. We will throw you out if we have to!" threatened Desikan through his clenched teeth.

Throwing back a menacing stare at Desikan, Amudan turned to his father and said, "*Appa*, I cannot leave this town. Find me any job in the town. I will take it up. "

"Don't listen to him, *Mama*. You get his bag. I will get the car," pushed Desikan.

"Stop that, Desika! You cannot take me anywhere. You will not understand. Stay out of this. Like how you usually stay out of the temple," muttered Amudan.

"For once, you stay off the temple! This is just a small town. Don't make it your world! Drive that into your head! This town does not need you. It will function the same way, even without you. Don't waste your time! Listen to me and for once, wake up and see the real world!" he yelled.

"Go through the grind, experience it, see it through and then come back here if you have to! Your Lord Amudan and this temple will go nowhere, remember?" He added.

"All right, Desika! I have heard enough. It's time to move on. I need to go back inside," muttered Amudan, his eyes glistening with anger.

"Desika, ask him to cut all the fuss and leave immediately. If he does not take up the job, tell him I will have nothing to do with him anymore. He will have no right over anything that concerns me, not even my last rites!" threatened Ramanujam.

Amudan merely stood staring at Desikan, cringing, and batting his eyes with impatience, choosing not to respond to his father's remarks.

"*Mama*, he will not listen to us. I will go and fetch Kumaran's father or Narayana *Bhattar*," suggested Desikan.

"Go! Go fetch anyone you want. Bring down the entire town, but you cannot dream of driving me out of this place A-L-I-V-E!" Swearing, Amudan walked back into the temple.

Ramanujam, mumbling abuses, turned with a huff and stormed towards his house while Desikan stood helplessly gaping around!

Amudan came out of the temple a long while later, after finishing his morning duties in the temple, supervising his men cleaning at the temple, minding the queue, and checking the stores of the *madapalli,* ensuring that the last man in the temple and the beggars outside were served the *prasadam*. He walked out of the temple carrying his palms full of *Ven Pongal*, knowing his friend would still be around.

Perching on the wall outside overlooking the temple pond, the two sat quietly eating the *Pongal* out of Amudan's hand.

"I cannot see you like this, Amuda! You run an institution here. For whose welfare? Lord Amudan's? No! He asks nothing of anyone, mind you! We only have to do our duty. Your duty is first towards your family to secure their future. Religion cannot rule your life, Amuda! Enough of this. Move out of here! These people here don't deserve you. They are merely using you. They have no respect for all that you are doing. You have only earned yourself all kinds of names. They will never understand you, Amuda!"

"What is there to understand? I am not doing anything for anyone. I am only doing this for myself, if at all. This is who I am, Desika. This is where I belong, where I am drawn to every waking moment of the day," he said as a stray dog ran over to him and stood wagging its tail.

Amudan dropped his hands down and the dog, resting his paws on Amudan's knees, lapped up his hands off the *Pongal* that was left over.

"I perhaps was a temple rat in my previous birth, still looking for my home and food within the walls here," mused Amudan.

"Your father has dreams for you, Amuda, and rightfully so. He literally begged me a few days back to make sure you leave for Mumbai. Can't you do this for him?" asked Desikan.

"Is that fair? Whatever you are asking?" pointed out Amudan. "Although your father will be more than pleased that you are even talking this way."

Without waiting for Desikan to respond, he went on, "Get on with your life, Desika. I belong here as much as you believe that you do not! There is no use forcing each other into things we cannot do," said Amudan, slowly turning to look at his friend.

The dog let out a bark, looking towards the road. Watching his mother approach, Amudan jumped out of the wall and sped to wash his hands with the dog running behind him.

"Amuda, why are you hurting everyone?" She walked towards them, yelling.

"Your *Athimber* had organised everything for you and even bought your flight tickets. You really don't care how upset he would be? Why didn't you tell *Appa* that you never planned to go? Why didn't you talk to your *Athimber* and explain? Why don't you at least make the effort to convince everyone?"

Amudan merely stood staring at her.

"Don't look at me like that. We have to make some compromises for the sake of the family. You have to learn to adapt. If all of them think that this job is good for you, you have to trust them and take it. If not, at least respect them enough to keep them informed of your decision. How could you stay quiet till the last minute and let us all down?"

"Didn't I tell you all that I don't wish to take up the job? That I don't wish to leave this place? You all can never hear me, Amma!" Amudan said in a soft tone.

"*Po da!*" she said with a click of her tongue. "You have a knack for complicating your life," she sulked, looking at him with concern.

"Here, eat this both of you," she said, smiling at Desikan as she handed them a box.

"Thinking my son is going so far away in search of a life, I made *Ksheerannam* today. His favourite dish," she said, wiping Amudan's face with the end of her *pallu*.

"You keep petting your son, *Mami*. He will not leave you and go anywhere," mocked Desikan.

He was not the first one to comment that way. It was the constant grouse of her husband as well, but could she help?

Ramanujam was a retired headmaster of the Government school in the town. A disciplinarian, a passionate educator, who took immense pride in his glorious tenure of service at the school, his past students, and their achievements. He gloated over every invitation for a student's marriage, housewarming, or business inauguration, or just an old student settled abroad calling on him.

Chemistry was his strongest obsession. While it quite let him down in his dealings with his son. An equation that forever was a daunting challenge!

Amudan was full of energy and extremely mischievous as a child. His mind whizzing with intrigue over things that his school textbooks hardly could keep up to. With his interests and learnings mostly lying outside of school, every day was a struggle for Amudan, being caged within the classroom for hours, with no purpose.

The weekend sculpting classes he undertook with the temple *Sthapathi,* with the sole mission of learning to carve out the image of Lord Amudan, were most engaging and turned into an obsession with time. If he were not at the temple, he would be spending days and nights sculpting, immersed in his craft, oblivious to the world around him. At times, he even missed his temple duties, knowing not what time or day it was!

Even after the whole town had fallen deep in slumber, the sound of his chisel and hammer would still go on up until dawn.

He needed no light, no rest, his hands kept moving, his eyes darting untiringly, his mind muted of all sense of pain. Stone after stone, his journey was unique. Moments of exhilaration, longing, the gruelling wait until the divine form slowly appeared on the stone. Like truth emerging out from the dismal depths of doom, like the first rays of sun piercing through the darkest room, the life and relief that came with it! Amudan lost and found himself each time.

He barely scraped through these school years, only to realise that education was way beyond his calling.

The blows he quietly took from his father for his poor scores or for bunking classes only drove this home harder.

It was a daily struggle for Perundevi and her daughters to protect Amudan from his father as he returned home from the temple. Ramanujam's day went by, a rigid schedule that he expected the rest of the house to follow, while Amudan followed that of the temple, only more diligently. He came home only after the *sayana aarthi* at the end of the day only to be received with cane blows. At times, he was even made to sleep outside the house when one of his sisters would sneak a pillow and blanket out for him.

Amudan grew more fearless and thick-skinned over the years. He learnt ways to distract his mind from the pain the wounds left. He held no grudge nor any remorse. If at all, he only felt more sympathy for his father at times, not being able to satisfy his father in any way.

Amudan tried to do all that he could to make it up to his father but only failed him more, while Ramanujam got more avaricious with time, determined not to give up on his son. The rest of the family suffered no less watching the father and son in their plights.

Ramanujam employing other means to get back at Amudan, one day threatened to throw away all the sketches, paintings and sculptures made by Amudan, after hearing of Amudan's abysmal performance in the tests prior to the board exams.

Amudan stood shocked, watching his mother in tears pleading with his father, gripping one end of the carton box carrying his works and begging him not to throw them away. Amudan scuttled in and out of his room and, holding out his chisel, said to his father, "Here, throw this one out!"

Much to Perundevi's relief, all of Amudan's works were sealed and saved in the attic. A few of the miniatures that she managed to smuggle out of the pile, she kept them buried in their rice drum. While Amudan never looked for his chisel again.

For once, he agreed with his father! Sculpting was indeed a fulfilling experience in itself. When he was led to discover the most peaceful and ecstatic state of his mind. However, he realised that it took much of his focus and time away from the temple service. The one thing he wouldn't trade off for all the pleasure there is in heaven or earth!

One other incident shook them all. It was during Amudan's school final year exams. The day before his last exam coincided with the beginning of the annual festival of the temple. Amudan hadn't come home the whole day and had also deftly evaded his father when the latter went scouting for him all around.

Until that evening, when the procession of deities began, Amudan stood there holding one end of the palanquin on his shoulder. Ramanujam's rage knew no bounds. Watching Amudan return home that night, he charged towards him, pulling out the iron spatula left on the *Dosa Tawa*, not realizing the stove was still on.

As Ramanujam raised his hand to hit, watching Perundevi come in the way to take the blow, Amudan firmly held the other end of the spatula.

Amudan bellowed in pain the next moment, as he cast the hot iron spatula aside. They watched him squirm and cuddle on the floor, holding his palm tight, tears gushing down his cheeks. His face had turned red in pain. They rushed him to the doctor immediately.

Ramanujam had a sleepless night, pacing up and down the house, watching over Amudan, calmly asleep. The sight of tears in his son's eyes made him choke every time it crossed his mind. He hated himself more for having spoilt his son's chances of even writing the last exam, with the right palm bring hurt so badly.

However, Amudan took them all by surprise by turning up at the exam hall on time but turned down the assistance for writing he was offered. What a painful three hours it was for Ramanujam to watch from far his son struggle to hold a pen and write! Any looks of concern, sympathy, or enquiries about the hand, from friends or teachers, were only met with a cold stare. That was the Amudan, they all knew. No one knew, though, what went on in his mind.

With that, the long years of his battle with books and all his classroom woes drew to a close. It was also the end of corporal punishments for Amudan! Finding it too distracting, Amudan dropped out of college, too.

From gardening to agriculture, plumbing, electrical or structural work, everything that had even the remotest bearing on the temple piqued his interest.

From toiling hard in the fields and keeping track of the harvest from the temple fields to the supply of haystacks to the temple *goshala*, he consumed himself over every small administrative detail. The cleaning of the temple premises, which started off as a weekend engagement with his friends, slowly grew into a daily regimen that he obsessed over. The temple authorities and *Archakas,* though, found his interference with every affair of the temple extremely annoying, they were forced to tolerate it for they knew he was also the one that each one of them could count on when in trouble. For who else would skip college to make sure the drainage block in the head priest's house was fixed or a snake in their backyard was caught in time?

Ramanujam's blood boiled at all this. He felt helpless, neither being able to tame his son nor the others who took advantage of him. He stopped going to the temple and for years now.

The Temple Rat

Amudan was the talk of the town in the days that followed.

Ever since the news of his moving to Mumbai for a job, the town went abuzz with curiosity. Every move of his was put through a wide spectrum of interpretation. His unfriendly demeanour, his authority, ways, and airs, which people found most intimidating, were now looked through a prism of sympathy. While many were relieved by the news, some found it hard to believe, and there were a handful of others who felt a tug at their hearts, imagining him away. All their eyes searched for Amudan every time they were in the temple. Now that they knew he had turned down the job, all their resentment for him returned only doubly strong.

He was not liked by most people. Amudan knew that better than anyone else and as much knew that he was more to blame. He shouted to be heard, to get his way. He was a terror for many, from the security guards, cleaners, gardeners, and administrative staff, to the junior priests serving at the temple and not to mention the devotees who regularly visited the temple. He ruled them by fear, more for convenience if not a cover.

What was more intriguing was Amudan's ability to easily make friends!

Being a man of few words, and with a not-so-congenial disposition, it was a wonder how Amudan connected on a personal level with different kinds of people from all spheres, be it rag pickers, municipality workers, local vendors, auto and cab drivers or the police patrol team, lawyers, doctors, and bank and government officials who visited the temple.

He had his differences with all of them and was quite vocal about it. His candour and unpretentious nature won their hearts always while his quick temper evoked much fear. They were careful around him, joked about him behind his back, but quietly rooted for him, even without their knowledge.

"*Anna*, how long do we all have to put up with this?" remarked Vasu *Bhattar,* to another senior priest of the temple, referring to Amudan howling at the milkman who had turned up late to the temple.

"He is no trustee, no office bearer, not even a devotee as far as I know, he does not contribute one penny to the temple *hundi*, yet he assumes the authority to drill each one of us if we enter the temple even a few minutes late," he added.

"Being just about half my age and younger than most of us here, how can he address us in this tone?" he went on fuming.

"I agree with you, Vasu. He is like a child to most of us here and also the one we all fear. So much that I don't wake up these days thinking of *Perumal*. Our Amudan is the first one who comes to my mind," replied the senior Bhattar, letting out a chuckle.

They fell quiet, watching Amudan carry a huge vessel of milk that he had freshly drawn from the temple cows with the milkman walking alongside pleading, "Amuda, I come here on time every day. My son was sick! That is why I was delayed today."

Amudan, quietly walked into the *madapalli,* placed the vessel, emerged out and walked away breezing past the milkman and the two priests staring at him.

He had his ways of wielding control over each one of them at the temple. Especially the temple staff and volunteers, who knew that if they were not available on time, their job would be done without them.

This man who couldn't memorise even a single line from his school textbooks, from the corporation cleaners to the temple trustees, had all their phone numbers sorted and stored in his memory. His father often remarked, "*His brain is so clean and empty, it's no surprise it can hold a directory of phone numbers now!*"

He was right. Amudan's mind was clean, and he imagined an uncompromisingly cleaner atmosphere around him. Litter-free roads and pavements and immaculate walkways inside the temple were his mission. Any devotee found dropping any litter around the temple would immediately be shown his way to the dustbin. Amudan had a team of volunteers to do this in his absence and even during festival times.

Through persistent efforts, he put in place a system of disposing of the temple waste, cleaning at frequent intervals to ensure every shrine, counter and corner in the temple was left pristine throughout the day.

This often drew much flak from all quarters. For, dealing with his obsessive ways of enforcement for the upkeep of the temple, drained every bit of the spiritual energy they could garner.

While Amudan commanded a dedicated team of volunteers, meticulously trained to carry out every task at the temple. All his practice of taming stones with a chisel came to his help, perhaps, in shaping many of the teenagers of the town into disciplined adults for serving at the temple. Amudan was quite an icon among the youth of the town. His looming presence, all-round ability, courage, curtness and command, instilled fear and awe. He grew on them, evoking much adulation in their hearts.

To be in Amudan's team was the dream of many of the younger ones in the town and, in fact, even some of their parents. For they all knew that the rigours of training under him would only mould their children stronger to face any challenge in life.

No spreadsheets, no elaborate team meetings, with just his plain, native ways, and uncanny ability to envision every minute detail with the precision of a sculptor, Amudan steered the activities and festivals at the temple with stringent time measures.

Some feared him, some abhorred his very presence, and many others denounced his ways, but the fruits of his labour, they all enjoyed, quietly every day.

Amudan sprang from his bed, waking up from a strange dream.

He dreamt of Goddess Komalavalli draped in a beautiful copper-sulphate-blue colour silk saree with a pink border, bearing the design of swans in it. He noticed a little rat biting the edge of the saree when he woke up with a start!

It was only three o'clock. He lay down, still musing over the dream that had shaken him. When he had dozed off again, the dream recurred but without the rat this time.

He dreamt of the Goddess seated on the swing in the *Navarathri Mandapam*, clad in the same beautiful blue saree. Amudan woke up a while later, thinking it must be the impact of the saree selection he had done a few days back from the weaver who regularly supplied to the temple. He couldn't recall seeing this particular colour though. While the thought of the nibbling rat in his dream kept him on tenterhooks all morning.

It was the beginning of the *Navarathri*, a festival of nine days celebrated during September-October. The temple was bustling with the preparations for the celebrations in the evening.

As Amudan and his team were decorating the *Navarathri mandapam*, he noticed a ray of blue flash past his vision. He instantly turned around and stood shocked, staring at the same blue saree that he had seen in his dream. His eyes scanned the saree from its fall to the top until they met Komala's. She stood bewildered, watching Amudan's strange behaviour. His look turned from shock to disappointment, holding her gaze for a moment like he had something to tell her, and then he turned away. After a while, watching Bhooma waltz past him, he called for her.

"Ask Komala where she bought the saree!" he said.

"Eh?" remarked Bhooma. She looked around, hearing some giggles from afar and watched Komala and her friends exchange smiles while looking at her and Amudan.

"Ask her!" he howled with impatience.

Walking up to Komala, she said, "*Anna* wants to know where you bought this saree?"

There was a burst of laughter at that. Watching Amudan still grim-faced and looking at them, Komala replied, "From Chettiar *Mama,* " stifling her smile.

Those moments as Amudan stood gazing at her as she entered, that fraction of a second when his eyes met hers before he looked away, evoked a spring of emotions Komala had never experienced before. Her hands and legs were cold and shaking like she was going to flutter away! Her eyes still flushed with passion, she tried hard to compose herself, the racing emotions and her quivering cheeks and lips.

She was only jolted by Amudan's loud voice.

"Do you bring sarees to the temple after you have sold your best ones to all the women in town? Do you bring leftovers to choose for *Thaayaar*?" he charged the vendor on a call.

Even as the senior man meekly tried to gather himself and his words, Amudan, in his explosive voice, said, "No one needs to tell me, *Mama*. I am seeing it for myself. The ladies of the town clad in the best of your collections! Did you think I will not know?" he yelled at a man almost three times his age.

Amudan wasn't aware of his surroundings, nor the tremor or the wounds his words were leaving. Bhooma stood agape, helpless, watching her brother in a rage. Kumaran rushed to Amudan and flicked the phone out of his hand as the latter followed him, still bellowing accusations at the saree vendor.

Komala stood terrified, watching the scene. She could hardly make out what was happening. Her eyes welling up, she dropped her head down in shame, trying to hide behind her friend. Just a moment ago, she was flying high, delirious with ecstasy and all of a sudden, she felt as though cast to the ground and almost disrobed with the whole world watching on. How she wished she could vanish!

Soon, the festivities took over. Watching the Lord Sarangapani and Goddess Komalavalli on the palanquins being carried to the *Navarathri Mandapam,* the unpleasantness of the past moments faded from all their minds. Komala was however still fighting her tears. The shock, humiliation and, on top of it all, the hurt of being misled, wrecked her mind.

She couldn't yet believe that the special moment meant nothing but a mirage! Neither could she drive her mind out of it, nor could she stop her eyes vainly reaching for Amudan.

Amudan was right before her, carrying one end of the palanquin on his shoulder, slowly walking the Lord and his consorts to the decorated swing area. He looked calm as the mid-sea. There was no trace of any bitterness or anger or the wild tide that had just swept by. She hopefully looked at him every time.

Not once did he look towards her. What a gnawing sting that it left her with!

She walked back home, his words still ringing loudly in her ears. There was an enormous relief as she undraped her saree. She shoved it aside with a resolve to never touch it again. That was the moment she felt the first spark of anger that soon spread like wildfire at Amudan, at herself and the Lord who stood witness to all that.

She wondered why in the first place she was even drawn to Amudan. Apart from being raised in the same town, they have had nothing much in common; she thought. She has seen him all these years, every single day! They almost grew up together, only a few houses away and have been an integral part of each other's lives so far, without a choice! It was strange how all through these years they had managed to preserve their identities. Watchful of each other and wary of their differences, they haven't even exchanged many words. If at all, she had only heard him howl at someone or cause a bustle of activity in the temple!

What's more, his sharp tongue, knows no distinction! His words fell like a sword on anyone and everyone. What worth or virtue could one find in him? He just roamed all around wild like a barbarian with a squad he commanded. They were all his clones who thought and acted like him, unkind, unemotional, buzzing around like machines, disrupting the quiet and tranquillity around the temple, with their loud voices and their noisier brooms. Her mind raging with these thoughts, she realised she only despised him more! That gave her some peace. She could finally muster some sleep that night.

The festivities ended, the crowd dispersed, the palanquins and the swing were all parked back in their places and the temple was cleaned up, ready for the next day. Amudan and the team, wrapped up, after a long day's toil, not to mention the futile hunt for a rat all day!

The drill

The incident at the temple left Bhooma sour too and very embarrassed. Amudan could sense that she was upset with him. Never spoke to him or answered him. He let her be.

Being harvest time, Amudan was busy in the fields most days. A passionate farmer and an advocate of organic farming, his learnings started very early on working in the fields of Kumaran's grandfather and trained by him on all the conventional methods of cultivation and fertilisation. With the passing away of Kumaran's grandfather, a portion of his fields were gifted to the temple by the family and continued to be managed by Amudan in all earnestness.

As a mark of a propitious beginning, Kumaran's father had Amudan sow the first seeds in the paddy fields belonging to their rice mill every season.

"*Your son was not born to just feed your family but the entire human race,*" he often said to Ramanujam and Perundevi. To the parents, the daily harvest from the vegetable garden in their small backyard was indeed enough proof of that!

Year after year, the paddy fields saw a rich harvest and delivered quality produce. The sight and touch of the black, alluvial soil, at the fields often brought back memories of his sculpting days. Sometimes he even longed to get hold of the chisel again!

Then, heaving a sigh, he would look around him, at the sprawling fields, the flourish and fullness of it only brought to his mind the majestic form of Lord Amudan and his magnanimous smile. While the river Cauvery jauntily flowing, her bounty and grace reminded him of the compassionate presence of Goddess Komalavalli. He didn't need a chisel anymore, he thought. His vision only kept growing vast and beyond, with time!

Whether he was working on the fields, his legs soaked deep in the soil or was riding along the fields on his bicycle basking in the breeze, the fresh scent of the soil and the sight of an unending sea of tall green crops waving, gave him a sense of abundance and joy like no other. The fertile soil, nourished by river Cauvery and all the expansive dense green fields around, was the wealth he dearly cherished, nurtured and strived to protect.

Agriculture was the principal activity of the town, the source of livelihood for many families, with an ecosystem of its own. Amudan's expertise in the field grew as much as his fame. Readily volunteering to help other farmers with his techniques and quietly influencing many others into shifting to organic methods, his span of control in terms of acreage grew inorganically.

Kumaran, through his connections, helped these farmers find a direct market for their organic produce.

With their infectious zeal and commitment, the two young men inspired many of the farmer's sons and daughters to take pride in their roots and pursue agriculture for a living and as a way of life!

Protection of the native breed of cows was an allied mission that Amudan and Kumaran committed themselves to, along with a few like-minded farmers.

With heavy dependence on cattle in organic farming for cultivation and fertilisation needs, Amudan and Kumaran set up a network with dairy farms to get hold of older cows that had stopped producing milk. They made sure these cows found a farmer's home, fed on the hay from the fields and provided their nutrient-rich manure for better yields, making way for a seamless self-reliant system.

Kumaran and his father encouraged and supported Amudan in these ventures and were as much benefited from his methods and experiments in their own rice fields.

Knowing Amudan was on it out of passion, and to ensure no one took undue advantage of it, Kumaran chipped in to fix the commercials with other farmers for Amudan's efforts in their fields. The commercial aspect being the last of his interests, and with Perundevi and Kumaran handling it, Amudan had not even the faintest clue of what his earnings were.

While Ramanujam was equally clueless watching Amudan coiled and asleep in front of his dinner plate, and wondered, "*What really drives this young man?*

To do all that he does in a day with all his heart and soul but without a dime in sight!"

True, who could get to the depth of a heart that dreams beyond oneself, or find the rewards of fulfilment that come from the toils in selfless pursuits? Indeed, there were not many who could understand Amudan.

Though it only pained Amudan more watching the ways of people around him, the struggle they endured in search of progress, moving far away from the hometown that had seeded all their dreams.

While stretched under the shade of a mango tree overlooking the fields, he often thought about his friends and wondered what their lives would be like. At times, Kumaran showed him pictures of their friends on their graduation, on their first day of corporate jobs, in fitted suits and matching ties. Amudan merely let out a faint smile. No one could tell what he thought of it all. For he only had one thing to ask of each one of them when they spoke: "When will you visit home?"

He couldn't still come to terms that their homes had all moved very far away. He could never understand that their career-blinkered lives have allured them to a different set of choices, commitments and necessities.

He couldn't accept that they had at some point traded off all their claims to the warmth and comfort of a modest town life and by their own choice!

"We cannot hold them back, Amuda," Kumaran would say. "We can build businesses and learning centres, but remember, we cannot dream of holding anyone back." He reasoned.

As much as Mother Cauvery enriched their land enough to yield more than they needed, even her copiousness couldn't contain the aspirations and desires of all those she fed. Like children deserting their aged parents for a better life, people moved out in droves to cities, other states, and countries.

Even the ones left behind, who, although couldn't shed their ties to the land, still looked at those from other cities and countries, with adoration and a deep sense of longing.

For Amudan, though, every empty home he saw was a painful reminder of all the people who had left the town, each one of them from his childhood or growing years, whom he vividly remembered. He had a picture of the town in his mind that he wished he could rebuild just the way it was with all the people in it. Even as he was dreaming, homes were changing hands, slowly replaced by shops, apartments, banks, computer and other training centres and sprouts of business houses everywhere.

There was a churn all around, and it was inevitable. He was barely learning to accept that and grew more fiercely protective over what was left.

If anyone, it was the volunteers at the temple, the *Sripadamthangis*, who were most subject to Amudan's emotional outbursts and exhortations. Even while initiating the training of the *Sripadamthangis*, he made sure each one of them prioritised the service and the temple, and their work and lives revolved around it. Wherever they were, they were expected to report for temple duty at the appointed time. Else, all hell would break loose!

"He is being too hurtful, Kumaran *Anna*. Even I am extremely disappointed that I could not make it on time for the procession today. When I call to inform him, why does he hurt me, saying, *'Don't even bother coming! Perumal and Thaayaar are not dependent on you!*'" lamented Gopal, one of the *Sripadamthangis* who, although working in Hyderabad, made it a point to fly down for the temple service during the festivals.

"Don't you know him, Gopal!" Kumaran tried to pacify.

"He should know, *Anna*!" cut in Gopal. "That all our lives are not the same! It is too much of a struggle at times and we were all not made like him. We are all far less privileged, to say the least. We are though trying our best, despite our circumstances and shortcomings. We don't need any appreciation, but at least he can be kind! We all come there for a few days hoping to forget about our mundane lives," went on Gopal.

"Let it go, Gopal!" Kumaran uttered softly.

"You don't take his words to heart. You know he will melt the moment he sees you. Come soon. Have a safe flight," said Kumaran, and they hung up.

Only Kumaran knew how much Amudan looked forward to Gopal's trips and what a lot of anxiety he went through till the time he heard that Gopal had boarded the flight and after the heated call with Gopal that morning, how many times Amudan had absentmindedly called every other volunteer "*Gopala*" all day. Like a mother awaiting her son's return, his eyes were always on the lookout, hoping Gopal would be there any minute.

Indeed, all his angst and anger vanished in a moment! Amudan spotted Gopal from far during the procession the next evening, as the latter rushed out of his house, in a hastily wrapped *Dhoti* and *angavastram*, sprinting towards them. As he came near, Amudan, bearing one end of the pole of the palanquin alongside Kumaran, nodded at Gopal, ushered him closer and let him take his place, quietly stepping aside.

What a sense of victory it was for the rest of the *Sripadamthangis* to witness this sight! Gopal choked with emotions, exchanging a smile with Kumaran standing alongside him.

There were not many other things that Amudan really cared for. His most cherished possessions included a bicycle gifted by his father for his fifteenth birthday, a mattress he had sewn by himself, out of recycled cotton dhotis of his father and his mother's sarees.

For Padma and Bhooma, it was always fascinating to see their mother's oldest and softest *Sungadi* cotton nine-yard sarees turn into a brand-new quilt or a handbag that he would gift them. Every piece of wood in the house was also ingenuously recycled to suit their needs. Perundevi could never stop gloating over the furniture that Amudan had deftly done up. She cleaned and wiped them every day, the most precious treasure that she wished to preserve for posterity!

Everyone who knew Amudan would know that wherever he was or whatever he was in the middle of, soon after the temple opened in the evening, he would be in the sanctum sanctorum, right before Lord *Aravamudan*, holding a large wooden-handled hand fan, and gently waving it for the Lord resting before him. Like it was his purpose, the most precious moments of life that he lived for!

In those few minutes of quiet and solitude with the Lord, everything around him was dazed out of his mind. He stood beguiled by the enormous presence before him, his hands moving rhythmically when even his breath seemed to have come to a halt.

Narayana Bhattar, the head priest, would walk in, careful not to shake the tranquillity of those moments.

Amudan, with a few deep breaths, would place the hand fan in its place and, taking the "*theertham*" and "*Shatari*" that Bhattar would serve him, he would tiptoe out of the shrine.

This was his prayer, penance, and a prize beyond reckoning! The elixir that healed, energized and enlivened him each day.

The rest of his day was full of action whether he was running behind a Temple Regulatory Board executive, pressing and prodding him for approval for any temple repairs, fighting over a budget allocation or pulling up a temple staff or volunteer, the drill and drone of it was quite a pain for those around to bear!

"Amuda, can you not sit quietly for a few minutes?" Govindan snapped, in between his reading of the Ramayana, quite rattled by Amudan on a phone call bawling at someone.

Given his eloquence and melodious voice, Govindan's reading of scriptures often captured people's attention and devotees would even sit by for a while just listening to it. It pained Govindan to think that Amudan was too involved in the mundane activities of the temple and that he was getting more and more impervious to the divinity around him. Even worse, he felt Amudan was more of a disturbance these days.

"Amuda, you and I were both raised in the same temple and by His grace, we are serving at the temple as well. We cannot act irresponsibly, shouting and fighting with people around us. You have to mellow down, Amuda, and learn to practice some decorum expected of the place we serve in. Isn't it? What is the point of it all otherwise? "

Amudan was listening intently.

"I know you like to listen to the Ramayana. Your mother has mentioned it to me. I will reserve a portion of my day to read the scripture and explain Saint Valmiki's words to you, line by line. Will you listen?" He asked, his eyes shimmering with hope.

Amudan, with a scoff, faintly nodded.

"Why are you smiling? I am serious. Shall we start tomorrow? It's an auspicious day," Govindan gently persuaded, looking at Amudan. He noticed a sudden change of expression on Amudan's face and the next moment...

"Where did you get those flowers from?" Amudan went charging at a devotee holding a ball of strung jasmine flowers.

Watching the lady fumble for words in fear, he asked again, "Where did you buy these flowers from?" Trying to sound calmer.

"At the shop outside the temple," she said hesitantly.

"Come with me! Give the flowers back to her. Why do you buy faded flowers for the deities?" he reproached as he led the couple back to the flower shop.

"Take these flowers back and give them back their money," demanded Amudan to the flower vendor.

The flower vendor, Malli, meekly stood up, saying, "I bought them this morning only, Amuda. What can I do?

It's very hot and the flowers fade soon in this season." She reasoned helplessly, turning to the couple for support.

"No! No! You should have bought them as buds then. You have to sell only fresh flowers for the temple. You give their money back and take your flowers!" Amudan goaded on.

"It's ok, *Ma*. We will not give the flowers in the temple. We will keep it," pacified the man and led his wife back into the temple, muttering abuses at Amudan.

Malli, her eyes red with embarrassment and anger, folded her hands together at the kind-hearted man with Amudan still looking on.

"Malli, you wanted to carry on the business that your mother had been doing. We fought with others to let you hold the shop. If this is the quality of flowers you will sell here, I will not quietly sit and watch," Amudan warned, and left.

When he came out of the temple after the *Uchikaala* Pooja, he noticed a group of townspeople standing around Malli, who was in tears.

The moment she saw Amudan walking out of the temple, she sprang up to her feet and howled at him, "Who are you to threaten me? What will you do? Will you throw me out? You have no right to interfere in my shop affairs. I know how to buy and sell flowers."

She yelled and abruptly stopped, watching Amudan approach closer, glaring at her.

Fearing his uproar, as the crowd slowly began to disperse, he said, "I will be going to the market in a while. I will get the flowers for the shop today. We will see if they fade tomorrow." He challenged and, not waiting for Malli's response, he scooted off to keep pace with Govindan, who was rushing past in a huff.

"You are beyond any reform, Amuda. Just leave! We will talk later," said Govindan. "*Rajasik!*" he muttered to himself, shaking his head in disgust.

"Where are you coming now?" Govindan asked with a chuckle watching Amudan still walking along. Govindan playfully forged ahead into his house and tried to shut the door behind him. He was left helplessly giggling as Amudan quietly forced himself through the door.

He had his ways of healing them all. In a manner so plain and gentle, like a breeze! While most of them bask in its comfort as a matter of right or routine, only a few would take a moment to notice and cherish it.

"Why did you wash all my clothes?" Bhooma came sulking as Amudan entered the house.

"What else can I do? You go on piling up unwashed clothes. I can't stand the sight of them. If you can't wash them daily, I will have to do it. It's my problem, right?" replied Amudan, relieved that she finally spoke to him.

"Right! That too, since you don't let us buy a washing machine!" she pointed out.

Then, with a reconciliatory smile, she added, "Anna, please, don't wash them," batting her doleful eyes, feeling sorrier for being cold to him for over a week now.

Komala was still hurting, though. In all her pain and anger, she could never notice the quiet efforts that went in to bring to her the most exotic flowers for her to string the garland each day. While she only knew Amudan as a bully, revolting at their drawing large *kolams* on the temple floors, she wasn't aware of the fit he threw when someone even accidentally stamped over her *kolam*.

As for Malli, there was never a day without a fight with Amudan over one thing or the other. That she had not opened the shop on time, that the tray she had lent to devotees to carry flowers to the temple was not clean or that she had not removed the hard stem from the *Tulasi* leaves.

She found herself battling every day, annoyed at the very sight of Amudan, but she as much knew one thing for sure. That he would never give up on her!

Clash and complexities

"Amma, I am very hungry," called out Amudan, breezing in.

As he washed his legs and entered the kitchen, he jolted, seeing his elder sister, Padma, standing beside his mother.

With a deep sigh and a faint smile, "*Akka*, when did you come?" he inquired.

"We came this morning, Amuda. *Athimber* has also come. He is very upset with you, *Da*. He has gone with my father-in-law to attend to some land matters. Why did you insult him, Amuda? You could have at least attended the interview for his sake."

Amudan, in a huff, turned and walked out of the house without paying heed to his mother, calling him back.

"He will come, don't worry, "Perundevi pacified her elder daughter, chiding her for bringing up a sore subject as the first thing to say.

Perundevi, knowing where she could find Amudan, walked all the way to the temple pond.

He was there, along with a couple of friends.

"Amuda, come home to eat," she commanded, dragging him aside.

" You should not hurt *Akka* that way. She means well. They both want to see you settle well in life. You cannot fault them for that, Amuda!"

"Amma, haven't we spoken enough about this?" He remarked with exasperation.

" I have told them enough that I am happy as I am. I don't know how I can convince them. While I don't see their point either. We keep dreaming of different things and seem to speak to each other in different languages. Only that, anything I say always makes her cry! "He said and paused. "She may not believe it, *Amma*, but I never want to see her in tears. This is the only solution I can think of, for now. Staying away! You attend to her, *Amma*. I will come home later," said Amudan.

"She is also feeling bad, Amuda, and is very upset that you left without eating," explained Perundevi.

"No, it's not her fault at all. Sadly, we cannot keep things from each other for long. We can only speak our minds as we think, even if it hurts. We cannot pretend to have nicer things to say! I will only hurt her, *Amma*, again and again..." he muttered.

"It's all right! She will bear with it," said Perundevi, holding an affectionate smile and went on, "She is waiting. Come, have dinner with her. Tomorrow she will go back to her in-law's place. Poor child, she hardly gets to see us all!" she coaxed as she led Amudan by her hand.

"Don't avoid me, Amuda! I will not speak about it again if you don't want me to," blurted Padma as they sat down to eat.

"Just one thing. Athimber wanted me to tell you that you can call him anytime if you change your mind and wish to take up a job in Mumbai. Will you?" She asked.

"I will," said Amudan, and asked, "Where is Sarangan?" enquiring after her son.

"He wanted to come with me, but since his *Thatha* wanted to show him their field, I sent him with them. He has been asking to see you since he got out of the car."

"*Amma*, has Bhooma eaten?" asked Amudan.

At which Bhooma sprang out of her room, asking, "*Anna*, how do I look?" Showing off her new attire.

He let out a wide smile with a glance at Padma.

"*Akka* bought this *salwar* for me. I will come with you for the *sayana aarthi* today. *Akka*, are you coming?" chirped Bhooma, full of cheer.

After a fulfilling *darshan* at the temple, the three of them sauntered back home with Bhooma filling in her elder sister with all the *Agraharam* buzz.

Walking down that road with Amudan and Bhooma by her side was all the cosiness of a home she could ever ask for.

Padma dreamily walked on, her eyes grazing over every familiar joint, like pictures from an old forgotten album. *Nothing much has changed,* she thought as she looked at the row of houses on either side of the road. Some of them petit, some huge, painted in colours of peach, yellow and cream, each one of them, even the ones now run down and deserted, bringing back warm memories of their growing years.

She halted, finding an empty *thinnai* of a locked home, led them to it and perched herself between Amudan and Bhooma. Lost for words, she sat aimlessly gazing at the passers-by, their gait and demeanour quite soothing to her eyes. She had gone very far from this life, she realised, just watching the town slowly wind down for the day. Amidst the clatter of the vessels from the house next door, she could vividly hear the lively conversation of a family over their dinner, and louder was the voice of Ranganayaki, the head priest's wife, two houses away, on a phone call, as it seemed, in the middle of one of her never-ending, life-counselling sessions!

She then glanced at Amudan, who was engrossed in inspecting the cracked roof tiles of the locked house with the flashlight on his phone. His lean physique, toned muscles, layers of sun tan, his dry, blistered feet, bearing every other mark of his daily hard labour!

She watched him on, his zestful eyes glistening in the dark with the curiosity of a child. Her worries took over, as always.

"Amuda, is *Appa* still not talking to you?" asked Padma. He shook his head, turning to her.

"Soon Bhooma will also get married and move out! You will be all alone, Amuda," she went on, unable to take her eyes off his innocent face.

"I know how passionate you are about the temple and your service there. That's where you grew up. We carry memories in our hearts but have to lead our lives. We cannot be the same persons we were when we were children. Everything around us changes and we evolve along with it. That is the norm of life. One day, even our parents will become memories. What will you do then, Amuda?" She asked, swallowing a huge lump in her throat.

He looked up and pointed to the temple *Gopuram* standing tall.

"This is what I dream of every night," he softly uttered and, after a long pause, went on. "I know all of you have dreams for me, but I only wish you could see through my eyes. I wish you could experience what I feel living through each day." She couldn't wait for him to finish.

"*Appa* is hurting every day worrying over you. Don't you have a duty to your parents? You cannot be complacent with the money you make here doing small jobs, Amuda. Do you know how much you need to run a family when it grows? Do you know how much you have to save for the future? Do you know how much a day's hospitalization costs? Do you think what you earn will cover all that? Do you have any worry about all this?" She piled on.

"I don't know any of this, but I do worry a lot. My worries range from whether the milkman at the temple showed up on time; if the latest born calf in the *Goshala* is feeding well; whether *Bhattar* mama remembered to lock up the safe after use, whether the provisions at the *Madapalli* are rightly stocked, whether the harvest this year would be sufficient," he said and took a deep breath, seeing her stare at him with disappointment.

"This is who I am, *Akka,* and this is my world. I am absolutely at peace doing all that I do here," he added softly.

" *Po da!* Do we all ever come to your mind?" she asked, her eyes slowly giving into tears. Amudan brusquely turned away, not wanting to indulge her more, his gesture reminding her of her son, barely six!

"You are our only worry now, Amuda. I prayed to Lord Amudan, asking him to give you back to the family. Our ageing parents need you. They want to see you settled in life. They have a right to that. Who will marry someone who slogs all day for the temple? It may not be important to you. "

"For my sake.." she began to say.

"You ask me for my life.." he cut in. "I can give it up without a fight, but don't ask me to move out of here, please! That will shatter all our dreams!" warned Amudan, looking right into her eyes. They fell quiet at that.

Watching Bhooma fast asleep behind on the *Thinnai*, Amudan in a hushed tone said, "You hear her talk on the phone for five minutes and count the number of times she utters the words "patriarchy", "privilege", "toxic" and one more word" gaslighting"! What is that? Just curious, as I have never seen her get near the gas stove anytime!" he whispered with a naughty glint in his eyes.

Padma trifling a chuckle, said "*Appa* made a mistake, Amuda. He should not have made you sit inside the classrooms. Even if you had overheard some of the lessons taught, you would have done us all so proud today." She saw his eyes light up with a smile.

One's relationship with God is something absolutely personal and unique. Some of us pray while in need. Some of us pray as a practice. Some of us never pray. This may come out of absolute accountability and confidence in one's own actions or out of sheer neglect, ignorance or the lack of faith in the power of the Supreme. Contrarily, it may also come out of complete trust in God, and faith in his will to steer the course of one's life. Like the blind trust, a child holds for its mother.

In happiness or woe, it is up to the mother to protect, heal and care enough to give only what the child needs.

For Amudan, on the other hand, his happiness, sorrow, anger or anxiety were all centred around Lord *Aravamudan*! With nothing to pray for, and no reward to seek, Lord Amudan and the temple were his blind obsession. An obsession beyond oneself that consumed everything else in him.

To the point that even if he were to be punished or banished for it, in hell or heaven, he would still choose to live no other way! Who was then, Lord Amudan to him?

If Amudan was proud of one thing, it was his name! That he was named after the Lord! Even as a little boy, when someone asked for his name, he would pat his chest with pride as he replied, "*Amudan*!" Nothing made him melt more than that one word! Who could understand him?

Given that his sense of security and belongingness came from nothing else, who could scare him with some woeful stories of penury or entice him with the fancy of a plush lifestyle? But he was young with his whole life ahead. Conviction and resolve, how long could they last, when pain and hard times strike? Indeed, no one can tell! All we know is that he was only being moulded stronger by the day, even without his knowledge.

"*Paah*!" exclaimed Kumaran, rubbing his head hard, after the bang of the *Shatari* on his head.

Vasu Bhattar nonchalantly walked past him, mildly gratified by the reaction, although pretending to have not noticed it.

Kumaran, still grimacing in pain, cast a dubious look around, wondering why it hurt him so much today. It didn't quite look to him that it was done on purpose.

The ecosystem around the temple was a heterogeneous mix of people.

Although they all were in service of the Lord, their expectations, their aspirations, their premise or even the plain of devotion were quite diverse and quite defined their relationship with the God they served and as much with one another.

Kumaran, coming from a different community and a wealthy background, elicited different reactions from the people around the temple. Some of them were unreservedly kind to him and welcoming, while others were unreasonably mean. There were those others who would oscillate between love and hate so frequently, *both without a reason,* he thought.

Most of all, his relationship with Amudan was indeed an eyesore for many. Call it jealousy or plain hatred, discrimination, insults and abuse in any form were all the weapons they used and those that Kumaran grew used to as well.

He walked over to a corner where he could sit, where no one would find him, and watched from far, the hustle over the *prasadam* distribution. It was at these moments that he found himself wondering if he belonged there at all. He could neither recite nor follow the hymns they recited or partake fully in all the religious exploits. He could neither mingle with the ones who were friendly nor look in the eye of others who only looked down upon him, their tuft and *tilak* more intimidating.

Amudan, in just a while, came looking for Kumaran, carrying a handful of the *prasadam* that was distributed, and perched beside him.

Reaching his hand out to Kumaran, he asked, "Why did you not wait for the *prasadam*?"

This quiet warmth, profound and pure, he could never find anywhere else. While eating out of Amudan's hand, he knew that this was the purpose he was there as well, and nothing else ever mattered more to him.

Unemotional, brash, and tough was how Amudan came across to most of them. Only a few could get past his hard exterior. What tenderness he bore as he waited, morning, noon or night for Kumaran, to share the temple *prasadam* with him!

These moments reminded him of the peace and comfort of his mother's warmth, whom Kumaran had lost when he was ten years old.

The temple was the home they bonded and grew up in. Without a doubt, it was Kumaran's attachment to Amudan that drew him into the temple fold. He hardly knew its religious sanctity, and all he cared about was to be beside Amudan in whatever he did. Whether he cleaned the temple premises or painted its walls, crafted little sculptures or worked in the temple fields. The more time he spent with Amudan in selfless service, there was an exalted sense of worth he felt and his wish to be like Amudan in every way he could only kept growing over the years. Quite to the amusement of his friends and family, he observed all the dietary restrictions as Amudan did and emulated his practices of hygiene and cleanliness in the deliverance of his temple duties.

Although people around him could only still see the differences, a few, including Kumaran's father, could perceive how far he had come! The shrewd, patient and level-headed human he was moulded into with a throbbing spirit, high morals and an unyielding commitment to the people of his town. Kumaran's father was grateful to Amudan for all this and more! If there was one weakness he had, it was Amudan, again.

It was a few days since the "*Shatari*" incident. Amudan was watchful of Vasu Bhattar and his snide remarks about Kumaran and his father, such as, "With *every politician they bring to the temple, whether the temple donations grow or not, their business for sure flourishes.*"

These remarks seldom affected Amudan, but he could sense all was not well just gauging the discomfort of Kumaran when Vasu Bhattar was around. He asked him if anything was wrong and Kumaran dismissed it, saying, "Nothing new."

Later one evening, while the devotees lined up for the *Theertham* and *Shatari* being served, he watched Kumaran squirm as the *Shatari* was brought closer to him. Amudan, just as the *Shatari* was to be placed on Kumaran, jut his head forward, taking the strike. Amudan shuddered in pain!

"Watch it," yelled Kumaran that instant, flashing a fiery stare at Vasu Bhattar while rubbing hard on Amudan's head. Vasu Bhattar stood agape, his hands trembling, watching Amudan's eyes blaze at him!

Deception

"Perundevi, read this letter and tell me what you would want me to do," said Ramanujam, handing over a letter from his friend.

He watched Perundevi read the letter, her eyes blooming with joy. She handed the letter back to him with a smile, saying, "Show it to Amudan. We can pursue the alliance if Amudan has no objection. The girl looks very cultured and they are a very good family too," she added.

"Definitely, but that is my worry, in fact. The girl looks very cultured, and the family is extremely good, but will all that suit our boy? Left to me, I will never look for a bride for him and embarrass myself. Who will marry someone who hasn't finished his graduation? He has no job worth the name. Why! I will not get my daughter married to a man like this! You tell me how I should reply to this letter."

Perundevi, with a sigh of despair, got up to leave muttering, "It's only better if you don't reply!" Turning back, she confronted her husband, "What is wrong with our Amudan? He may not have finished college, but he is more experienced than most of the students you have taught. He may not have a job with one title, but he works harder than most of the boys his age. He even earns enough to sustain a family, if you didn't know! More than anything, no girl can find a more virtuous man than him, mind you!"

Ramanujam intervened with his loud laughter and replied, "I can only pity you, Perundevi! As always, you are blinded by your affection for your son. I can't blame you! You were always proud of him, weren't you? Proud of all the apprenticeships he has undergone, from the temple footwear stand keeper, the carpenter, to the sculptor! I admit I can't even remember the full list! Now what is he, a farmer?" He raised his voice and paused with a look of disgust at his wife.

"Our maid was saying the other day, "*All the boys of our town have moved to other countries. If only our Amudan could have studied well, he would also be in America, wouldn't he?*" I am only appalled by your innocence. Anyway, give the letter to your son and ask him to respond."

It was one of the relaxed mornings at the temple, with not much of a crowd. Govindan seated before the altar of Goddess Komalavalli was reading the Ramayana while Amudan and Kumaran were finalising the statement of accounts for a temple festival that had gone by.

Bhooma came running and held out a cover to Amudan, saying, "*Anna*, I think it's something urgent. *Appa* wants you to read this letter and send a reply to Raju *Mama*. He said you do not have to show him your reply and that you can send it by yourself."

Puzzled, Amudan immediately opened the letter and read it earnestly until the end, when he broke into a titter. He looked up at Kumaran and Bhooma.

"Why is Raju *Mama* troubling *Appa*?" he said, handing the letter to Kumaran with a mischievous grin.

Intrigued, Bhooma and Kumaran tore into the letter holding either end of it.

"She is so beautiful, *Anna*! What are you going to say?" asked Bhooma, her eyes glowing with hope. "*Appa* must reply to it, isn't it? Why is he asking you to do it?" she asked. When Amudan with a scoff said, "He perhaps wants to see if I can read and write."

Watching Govindan helplessly looking at all their faces, "It's an alliance for Amudan," declared Kumaran with a wink.

Taking the photo and the horoscope from Bhooma, Amudan said, "Govinda, here, take this. Place it at *Thaayaar*'s feet and give."

Govindan immediately sprang up to his feet and took the horoscope in his hands. He walked to the altar, placed the horoscope at the feet of the Goddess, performed an *Aarthi* with all obeisance and returned carrying the horoscope with flowers, *manjal* and *kumkuma prasadam*. He handed them to Amudan with exhilaration, saying, "I was reading the chapter of *Sita Kalyana* from the *Ramayana*. To my mind, you have indeed received the blessings of *Thaayaar* on this."

"This is God sent!" he whispered, pressing Amudan's hands tight.

Watching Amudan still blankly stare at him, Govindan went on, "Don't hurt your father's feelings, Amuda. Be glad there is someone to look out for you who wakes up every morning with the hope you will settle down someday. It's no joke!"

Thus, saying Govindan sat back to resume the reading of Ramayana. Bhooma, who was still reading the letter all over again, dreamily smiled on hearing Govindan's words.

While Amudan was immersed in thoughts ruminating on the contents of the letter and Govindan's words.

Bhooma hesitantly handed the letter to Amudan, asking, "Will you surely write back to them, *Anna*?" Amudan nodded with a faint smile. Hearing a friend call for her, Bhooma sped away.

Bhooma's excitement over the alliance for her brother was unquenchable. Govindan's words instilled immense faith that things were taking a positive turn on the matter. Given that he had the timely blessings of *Thaayaar* on it, she was quite certain Amudan would act on it. His expression only strengthened her belief. Although she didn't discuss it with her mother or sister, she couldn't hold it to herself as well.

"*Akka*, will you pray that this should go well for my *Anna*? He should be happily married and settled soon, "she said to Komala, taking her into confidence.

A friend she trusted the most and whose prayers she believed would never go unanswered. Komala took in the words with poise. She prayed as she was told but could not hold back her tears as she stood before Lord Amudan.

"I can hide my feelings from anyone, but how can I hide them from you?" She thought and prayed for the Lord to cleanse her mind, as well, of any desire or ill will.

A few days passed by. It was the day of *Ratha Sapthami*. It was among the most celebrated festivals when devotees from nearby villages and towns thronged to watch the festive procession of the Lord with his consorts. A day that abounds with unparalleled cosmic verve, when the Sun God takes a turn towards the northern hemisphere. Also celebrated as *Bhishma Ashtami*, marking the auspicious occasion when the great warrior *Bhishma* from the *Mahabharata*, attained the Lord's feet.

On days like these, Perundevi never ventured out to the temple. For one, traversing through the crowd and queues was not the temple experience she savoured. She would rather await the Lord at her doorstep during the procession. As much as she knew that Amudan would never drop by home even to eat, for Perundevi, spotting Amudan at the temple on festival days was something she dreaded even more.

She would only fast and pray that Amudan was safe, wherever he was, whether he was working under the scorching sun, at perilous heights, or with a soaring temper all through the day.

The festive spirit, though, was all over! Komala and her friends were busy decorating the temple entrance with a massive *Kolam*. There was a team of young students of Govindan reciting the *Vishnu Sahasranama*, a collection of 1000 names of Lord Vishnu, as told by the mighty warrior *Bhishma* to King *Yudhishtra* in *Mahabharata*.

It was a practice Govindan had initiated, for *Vishnu Sahasranama* to be chanted at the temple by his students from dawn to dusk on this day and open for devotees to join in the recital at their convenience.

Komala was very enthusiastic about the group recital and being a weekend, she joined the chanting along with her students taking turns. After the morning procession of the Lord, there were quite a number of people who joined, their voices in unison resonating across the temple walls. Alas! Louder than all their chant was Amudan's cry, as he yelled, "Pick it up! Now!"

His roar reached up to the sanctum sanctorum, shaking every one of the devotees in the queue waiting to have the *darshan* of the deities and those ardently chanting.

As Komala turned to look in that direction, she saw Amudan taking on a senior man in the queue who meekly picked up a plastic bottle from the floor, mumbling abuses.

Amudan barged in, leaving all the devotees rattled, and forcefully led the man out of the queue, asking him to drop the bottle in the bin outside. A seething rage, unprecedented and shocking. Even the volunteers around stood aghast.

It sent a chill down her spine, seeing Amudan react so wildly. His callousness at a senior man pained her most. She wondered why no one in the queue raised a voice in support of the old man. Most of them were clueless as to what was happening and the others were in a state of shock.

Komala, with the glumness and distaste it left her with, couldn't chant a word more. She quietly sat with her eyes shut, focusing her mind on the voices around relentlessly chanting. Calmness eventually filled her breath.

That evening, the festivities at the temple resumed. Amudan was his usual self, dishing out instructions and overseeing the arrangements.

The bitterness of the incident in the morning was still lingering in their thoughts. The temple volunteers who stood witness to it and those who learnt about it kept their distance from Amudan, partly out of fear and mostly out of deep disgust.

Later that evening, Komala stood before her house, welcoming the Lord and his consorts in procession, majestically perched on the *Vahana*.

Her eyes involuntarily fell on Amudan, standing in front, bearing one end of the palanquin pole on his shoulder, his face at ease and the *Thiruman Sricharanam* on his forehead shining brighter than all the lights around. She batted her eyes away at the sight.

Can those symbols of divinity he bore on his forehead ever hide the savage mind beneath? Have all his years of loitering within the binds of the temple been in vain? Not a tinge of divinity ever percolated into his being? On what merits does he claim to get near and serve the Lord? Who is he trying to fool, the deities perched on his shoulders?

She looked at the Lord with despair, with another wave of thoughts rushing in. *Does your mercy have no bounds at all? Are you so blind to all our faults?*

At that moment, she was filled with gratitude, looking at the Lord approaching closer. *You have indeed protected me from going astray! What a fool I was to harbour feelings for a man like him! I was the one who was blind, not you!* With tears in her eyes, she offered the flowers to the Lord and his consorts standing before her. Her heart felt at peace.

Komala was not alone. Every other person in the town was invariably talking of the day's incident, different versions of it. Even the most benign of them, stoking the flames high. None of them knew the senior man who was shunted out, yet the mere ghastliness of the act shocked their conscience.

A spoilt brat, they called Amudan, blaming Narayana *Bhattar* and Kumaran for indulging him this far. *They will one day realise they were feeding a snake when he finally bites them,* they cursed. *This shouldn't go unchecked,* some roared! *Perumal is watching everything,* they whined. *He is an embarrassment, a curse to the town,* others claimed. A few of them sympathised with Ramanujam and Perundevi, concluding, "*They don't deserve a son like this*!"

From all the icy stares and snide comments, Amudan could quite sense the uneasiness around. He could gauge that his actions have upset them all, especially watching some of the volunteers, his teammates, in huddled-up conversations and others cautiously avoiding him. It was not a very unfamiliar feeling to him, being alone in his fights, disliked, denounced, or disowned for his actions.

He as much knew each one of them- the volunteers, particularly. What they loved, when they hurt, what wore them out, what cheered them up and what could break them! He even could tell when they were hungry. *Now, they were all angry at him and punishing him*; he thought and quietly bore with it.

He never once stopped to wonder as to what they really saw in him, never knew how much he influenced their thoughts, their personalities and how shattered they were in moments like this, lost and trying to pick up and put back together every piece of his image they held and their faith in him.

He was the man who uncompromisingly commanded each one of them to do the right thing only. Whose outbursts instilled fear but were never bereft of mercy or restraint, and whose motives were never to shame or discomfort another. But his actions that morning left them in a blur, as to what was real and what was not. While he left them to their struggle, quite oblivious to it!

When all the festivities ended, the temple almost deserted, when the *Archakas* and volunteers were barely left with the energy to drag themselves home, they watched Amudan scuttle around, taking a final stock of the utensils and supplies for the next day, checking if every shrine in the temple, the pathways and entry points have all been locked, picking up the last grains of litter on his way. Until finally, when the temple's main entrance door was drawn shut, they saw him walk away from there, all alone, as tall, untarnished and fresh as he had entered!

"It was a plastic wine bottle!" Amudan revealed when Kumaran raked up the subject a few days later to assuage the angst of many. Kumaran shook, watching Amudan's eyes as he uttered those words. *Like a wild cobra with its hood up and hissing!*

Bells chime

"This is an alliance that has come for you, Amuda. I cannot see it as a prospect for myself," bleated Govindan.

"It has not come for anyone. I have not met the family or the girl. It has only been referred by a common friend. That's all. The letter also mentions that they are a family who have been in temple service for three generations and," *Mr Vasudevan is very keen to get his daughter married to someone serving at the temple,*" Amudan read out from the letter.

"Given the educational qualification of the girl and the family's background, who else can be more suitable than you?" He reasoned and, noticing Govindan still wearing a hesitant expression, Amudan said, "You think this over and let me know if you would like to proceed with it. We can suitably respond. If you are not interested, I will only be sending back the girl's profile and horoscope with the *prasadam*."

"What will your parents think about me? I also want to see you married and settled as much as they would want to. "

"All that we will see later! Tell me, would you like to see the girl?" asked Amudan, holding out the girl's photograph. Govindan shook his head but at a glimpse from the corner of his eyes, he was drawn, glued and couldn't rein in his eyes from the portrait of a beautiful girl in the picture.

"That's enough. I am sending the picture back as well," said Amudan, stifling a smile. He slid the picture back into the cover, watching his friend blush.

Ramanujam was deeply upset to learn from his friend a week later that Amudan had written back, thanking him, saying, "I am sending the profile and horoscope of my friend, Govindan. More qualified in every way and a suitable match for Mr Vasudevan's daughter. I request you to take as much interest as you would in my case and pursue it. Thank you, *Mama*. Sending *Thaayaar prasadam* along."

The bride's family developed an instant liking for Govindan and they were pleased beyond words to learn that Govindan and their daughter, Sowmya's horoscopes, matched. Narayana *Bhattar* took the lead on Govindan's side and the marriage dates were fixed.

Bhooma was the hardest to handle. Throwing a fit around the house, blaming her parents for not seriously pursuing it and cursing Govindan for taking advantage of her brother, she was constantly on the phone with Padma. Hoping it would calm her nerves, she decided to spend a week with her sister, while preparing for her exams.

Bhooma returned home, only more angry and upset and for many more reasons now.

In a few months, the families of the town attended the grand wedding of Govindan and Sowmya held in the bride's native place.

The newlyweds were welcomed back to their little nest in *Thirukudanthai,* their hearts full of dreams. Govindan resumed his services at the temple right earnestly. His life, though, wouldn't be anything like before he realised with every passing day.

Sowmya, having been accustomed to the comfort and opulence of her parent's home, the complete lack of it in her life now came as a shock and in waves. Carried away by her love for Govindan and more enchanted by the abundance of his virtues, his soft nature and affectionate ways, her mind treaded less on what they lacked. But for how long?

Not knowing the difference between what a luxury to them was and what was a necessity or what was within their means and beyond, she struggled to come to terms with her life. She was young, and her aspirations only grew with every passing moment. She wasn't willing to be bogged down by her current situation. She was determined to grow beyond it, to dream beyond it and lead her husband into that part of a world he had never seen! She surrounded herself with friends and family who fanned her dreams or who were living the life she was dreaming of and treated all others as inferior or insignificant.

Amudan for sure fell in the second category. Although she knew that he mattered to Govindan the most, like a brother, like a father, as Govindan often said to her, she was determined to put him in a different place. She was very careful with her ways. She addressed him respectfully but treated him quite contrarily.

It all started one day when she constantly kept calling Govindan on the phone, knowing well he would never answer her calls while he was in the temple.

"Amuda, are you free?" Govindan called out to him, frantically stepping out of *Thaayaar Sannidhi*.

"Sowmya has called me many times. Can you go home and see if she needs something?"

Amudan went immediately.

"*Anna*, he forgot to fetch water from the well for cooking. He never lets me do it. It's ok, *Anna*. I will manage today," she said with disappointment. Amudan quietly fetched the water from the well.

The next day she called Amudan directly and from then on it became a part of his routine. For every errand or repair or to move things around the house, she knew whom she should call, while she said to Govindan, "When I have a brother to do everything for me, why would I even call you?"

Govindan was smitten. He took her words at face value and he knew Amudan would do all this for anyone and, of course, anything for him.

Ranganayaki's *thinnai* sessions with the neighbourhood ladies got more fodder now. From elaborate discussions about the colour and texture of Sowmya's drapes, her pompous gait to casually commenting on and reeling out every sensitive, confidential trivia even remotely concerning Sowmya's family, with an unwavering air of authenticity and with absolutely no qualms, Ranganayaki revelled in all the attention, she could garner.

Seating herself on the *Thinnai* at the entrance of her house, a coign of vantage that gave her a view of every passerby, Ranganayaki drew each of them into a conversation with her ever-disarming smile and irresistible warmth.

A neighbour, hawker, or a first-time visitor to the town, no one could escape her notice or walk past her unreckoned.

As Komala often mocked, "It is a one-way path! Even those who have migrated out of the town generations back cannot still find a way out of my mother's trap."

She was like a master sorcerer, enchanting people with her words. The tentacles of her memory could stretch any far and until they found a common connection with an acquaintance she just made. With that, she would cast her spell, smash down their guard and from then on, they held no claim or control over what they could reveal or what she could draw out of them, even those slipping out of their subconscious minds!

Ranganayaki was a repository with whom many trusted their secrets. She only left everyone more baffled at her recall. Like a grandmother's old trunk, it was a place where they could find the trinkets and treasures they had almost forgotten for years!

To their delight or dismay, it was always there, fresh as it was left!

All said, her empathetic ears and resourcefulness were indeed an immense source of strength to many ladies in the town. They could pour their hearts out to her without restraint. Whether she chided, mocked, or guided them, these heart-to-heart conversations were nothing short of a therapy to them. It was intriguing, though, as to what these daily huddles meant to Ranganayaki.

There were topics trending now and then, but ever since Govindan's marriage, Sowmya ruled over everything else. Not to mention the literally jaw-dropping moments watching Sowmya walk towards *Bhattar*'s home while they were deep in the middle of such a sensational subject when Ranganayaki deftly buttered up with a warm smile, saying, "Come, come, my dear, I was just thinking of you!"

Sowmya's dismissive glance around swept the rest of them away in a go while she haughtily perched herself beside Ranganayaki, her rightful place, as she reckoned for nothing less than a private audience she deserved.

There were many things they discussed, though Amudan was the point where they converged. Indeed, they had quite a lot of notes to share, and views to toy with, on that.

When once talking of Amudan's helpful disposition, Ranganayaki said to Sowmya, "Poor one, no one will help us all, as Amudan does. He will not take any money even if you offer. I only insist and make him sit and eat at times."

The condescension in the tone quite pleased Sowmya, though it was a mere manner of speech for Ranganayaki. Not many would know that the latter steered the conversation less to convey her mind but more to gauge that of the listener.

Ranganayaki often pondered over her husband's remark *"Your tongue keeps swaying all day, praising and criticising the very same people. I am curious if you even know what you really think of them?"*

She candidly observed people, brutally assessed their actions, and brashly spoke of them. She was unequivocal and consistent in her approach, though, so much so that even her husband was not beyond it!

"*Your father knows nothing*!" was all that Komala had heard her mother say in rebuttal of Bhattar's take on anything. His piety and personage, all slain in a lap!

After all his vain efforts to change her ways or tone them down, Narayana Bhattar could only sympathise with his wife, thinking," *She only tries to amuse herself with all the noise!*"

If there was someone who could disquiet Ranganayaki, leave her unsure of herself and fumbling for words, by his sheer appearance, it was Amudan! Nothing rattled her as much as his stoic silence! It was a heartening sight for anyone, to watch her swivel and rise to her feet, dropping all that she was doing, and go limping behind Amudan whenever he entered their house.

She would plead and hound him all along, listing out all the things she needed or those to be fixed in the house, as if it were her last chance of survival. Until she would finally ploy to make him sit through at least two fistfuls of the food she had cooked. She would then emerge out exhausted like after a day-long hard toil! While others would call her a hard taskmaster, Amudan always felt that her primal task was to have him fed.

Having said that, Ranganayaki and Sowmya still found an ally in each other in more aspects than one. Ranganayaki was only kinder to Sowmya, for she saw traces of her younger self in Sowmya that she loved to observe more. While Komala couldn't stand even the utterance of Sowmya's name in their household.

Perundevi and Ramanujam, without a choice, bore with all versions of these town talks they heard, particularly about Amudan, until it came as a blow one day.

When they watched Amudan rush in the middle of his lunch after Sowmya had sent a word for him that a water pipe in their backyard had broken and they weren't able to close the valve.

"Did you see what he has brought himself down to now?" remarked Ramanujam in shock. "Even if we had raised a cow, we could have had it tied in our backyard, claiming it was ours only. We have lost all our control now. Your son has lost all his self-respect." He bawled.

"Blame yourself for that!" retorted Perundevi.

"Watch your words, Perundevi! Whatever I did was only for his well-being and only to make sure he was not in the spot that he is today!" yelled Ramanujam.

"No! You took away too much from him! You made him feel that you don't love him as much as your daughters. You made him feel he was not as good as them. He accepted it as it is. He accepted you as you are. He thinks to this date that it is his fault that you are not as loving to him as you are to your daughters or his friends. You took away his pride!" She thundered.

"He once, as a child, asked me, "*Why is Appa not smiling at me, Amma? He smiles at Akka or Bhooma!*" He never understood why," she mumbled, choking with tears.

"Perundevi, please! Do you believe that? That I don't love him as much?" Ramanujam squawked in disbelief.

"I don't, but he was just a child then!" She cried. "Very inquisitive and playful. You wanted him to only study, obey, and be like others.

You took away all his sketches, his chisel, all the sculptures he made. You beat him up so hard!" She couldn't go on. She closed her eyes and cried aloud. She could no longer even bear the memory of those traumatic days.

"You could have starved him of anything but your affection. You could have shown a little of the love you showed for your daughters. Any amount of the excess I tried to give him could not make good of that. He still never blamed you! Thanks to you, one thing he understood is that not all people will love him. He has learnt to live with it. He is today even stronger than any of us. He has learnt to help anyone and everyone, unmindful of what they think of him or do to him. I am not sure many in this town have understood his value. They all will, one day! Every one of them!" She roared, her voice throbbing with emotions.

Wiping her tear-filled eyes with the end of her saree *pallu*, she breathed, "I only hope, in your lifetime, you realise that as well. How much he cares for each one of us! How much he respects you!"

There was not a day she didn't pray to Lord Amudan to heal the child as she dressed his wounds. While there was not a night, Ramanujam could go to sleep without worrying about his son. He lay mulling over his wife's words that night and drifted off to sleep as he prayed, "*If I have done things the wrong way, punish me, but not my son.*"

The Waves and Tide

While different people had different things to say about Amudan, each one with a contrasting take on his actions, speculating over his life and choices, truth be told, Amudan never had a moment or a thought to spare for himself. In short, he never took himself too seriously. He didn't care much if he was right or wrong but never ceased to explore anything that intrigued him, put his heart and soul into every little thing he did, and as much as he was aware, he never let himself be bound by what others thought of him. Like an experienced driver, deftly manoeuvring a vehicle through a chaotic stretch, aware of noise and movement on all sides but never intimidated by them.

Komala was quite the opposite. Extremely principled in her approach and a perfectionist by nature, even a minor slip from her expectations of herself or of others ruffled her a lot and gave her sleepless nights at times. Being a history teacher at school, her rumination over the subject continued even after school hours and beyond her classroom. Given her knowledge of the works of *Azhwars*, she often engaged in debates and discussions and documented her research works on the times of the *Azhwars,* the history and social conditions that prevailed then and their relevance to the present day. She scripted skits for her students, wrote columns in weekly magazines and contributed to research papers. On weekends she spent hours reading and writing at her favourite corner in the four-pillared *Mandapam* right before the shrine of Goddess *Andal.*

The sight of the temple during the twilight, the pathways being lit up with rows of oil lamps, people lining up in queue for *darshan*, the placid movement of those piously engaged in *pradakshina* around the shrines, the murmur of chatter here and there, and the gentle breeze carrying the tranquilising scent of *Tulasi* leaves and the fragrant flowers. Amidst the permeating divine aura, Komala sat immersed in thoughts.

Her quiet was disturbed by a loud conversation from the other end.

"History taught in schools is flawed, I hear, Amudan. Is that true?" asked one of the temple staff, finding Komala within earshot. Amudan was busy wrapping threads around a fire torch. Seeing him not respond, a senior *Archakar* beside him commented, "Why are you asking, Amudan? How would he know? Even his school principal used to be in the temple all day looking for Amudan!" At which, Amudan coyly smiled and Komala could hardly resist a snicker.

"Good for you, Amuda. You didn't miss much. Now they say much of our history is lost and what they teach in schools is all wrong. Now history teachers are all busy reading and finding the real history, it seems," added the temple staff with a sly glance at Komala.

Piqued by his shallowness and flippancy, Komala sat squirming with rage.

When another *Archakar* casually added, "It is nothing new, *Swamin*. Didn't the demons, *Madhu* and *Kaitabha* take away the Vedas long back? Vedas are the most ancient historical records available to mankind. There is no originality in anything we find these days, *Swamin,* not even thefts and frauds!" commented the Archakar.

"The times are worse now, aren't they?" chipped in the senior *Archakar.* "We at least could distinguish and spot a demon then. Now they are all masked as humans, more deceptive and dangerous! Our children have to be made aware of all the devious devices employed in the past and the methods of conquering them. They have to know all the battles of *Dharma* fought in this land in every century and how they were won or lost. They have to know in a clear light what was right and who was wronged, the politics behind and the outcome of it! More than anything, they have to know the value of *Dharma* and the sacrifices made in the past to protect it. History is truth, the bare facts! That is what is being denied," replied the senior Archakar.

Komala could hardly keep her head down with the turn their discussion was taking.

"Who cares about all that, *Swamin*? If survival is what our children should learn, they will still learn it from their circumstances and experiences. They don't need the history books for that. Their instincts will do. Let them teach whatever they want! We should not plant these doubts and confusion in their minds. This is the day's reality and they should face it and evolve with it. We cannot sit and brood over what is lost, "retorted the temple staff with nonchalance.

"What are you saying?" squawked the senior man. "If your children will learn by instincts, why send them to schools at all? Send them with Amudan to the fields. Let them learn to survive!" he said gruffly.

With a smirk, the temple staff went on, "How long can they survive in the fields? Machines are slowly replacing men everywhere. They need to learn to make and run those machines. That's what we send them to school for! That is evolution!"

"It is only delusion," cut in the senior priest. "In the name of progress, we are ready to accept and settle down for anything. We are ready to forgo truth, our own culture, and even our identity! Whatever progress he may make, your son has to still eat only what is produced in the soil. He cannot eat the machines he would make, I hope!" he spoke in anguish.

"At least, I wish I don't live to see that day!" He added while gently patting Amudan's shoulder, who was still engrossed in oiling the fire torch to be lit.

"Amuda, will our *Perumal* take another *avatar* to save us from the fools who believe in machines over fellowmen?" exclaimed the senior *Archakar* pressing his hand on Amudan's shoulder to rise to his feet.

"Looks like Goddess *Andal* will come to save this time," replied the temple staff, pointing towards Komala with a mischievous grin. Miffed and shocked at his audacity, she shot him a fiery glance.

"Komala, why are you reading in the dark, child?" asked the senior *Archakar* to lighten the moment.

"Like you rightly observed, we are all in the dark only, *Mama!* Only our *Perumal* should show us the light...!" Before she could finish, they all hooted in fear, watching the fire torch in Amudan's hands go ablaze, the fire almost brushing over the men.

Amudan, with a titter, calmed them, saying, "It's the wind!"

"Oh, I thought it was the END!" quipped the senior *Archakar*. With a roar of laughter, they all dispersed. Komala scooted away, giggling.

Komala was excited all through that night, recalling the incident. Especially, Amudan's face, lit up with a playful smile and a blazing fire torch in hand. For the first time, she noticed something gentle and warm about him. She felt a strange heaviness swamp her heart at that moment. She had fewer friends these days whom she could open her heart to. Most of them had left the town and there were others she couldn't anymore deeply relate to.

However, there were many around only to taunt her for who she was or the choices she made. She was just a redundant history teacher to them!

When education is itself seen as a mere means for a livelihood and attainment of materialistic goals, indeed it is a failed cause! She realised she was fighting a lone battle if not a lost one!

Watching Amudan only reminded her more of her loneliness. Though there were moments like that evening when it was a balm just knowing that he was still around. Like fire, water, earth, wind and space! Like her *Perumal*- her constant! Her eyes welled up with tears at the thought.

Everyone's life goes through a churn. Komala knew it was imminent for her as well. What's more, her mother was threatening her with the subject of marriage at every given chance. She felt like a stranger in her own house.

The temple was her haven, indeed. Lord Amudan, her only friend. Whether she was reading history, teaching or writing, her devotion to the Lord was steadfast. Like an unflickering light in the dead of night, it was her strength, her succour!

A few months passed.

"Amuda, my father wants to sell our house in *Thirukudanthai*. Padma mentioned that you had recently helped sell a house to a friend of yours, settled abroad. Can you find us a buyer?" asked Ranganathan.

"But.. why?" asked Amudan.

"It's a very old house, you know. Now with *Amma* and *Appa* moving in with us, we hardly get to stay there and cannot maintain it as well," replied Ranganathan.

"We can have it repaired and put it to use. It's among the very few old-styled houses in the town. We can do it up, just the way it is. I saw a place in *Tirupanandal* where they were trying to build old-styled village houses as a homestay for tourists. Your house is ideal for that, isn't it?" propounded Amudan, thinking aloud.

"Sure. If you think so. Would you like to take it up?" Ranganathan asked hesitantly, knowing Amudan had worked on a few other houses that way.

"Yes. A builder friend of mine usually helps me on these," replied Amudan and assured to revert with an estimate of time and cost.

Ranganathan was more than pleased with the deal while Ramanujam brushed it down, saying, "Amudan never easily lets anyone sell their properties. He convinced a colleague of mine to hold his house as a holiday home. He then set up a vegetable garden in their backyard and kept sending them the weekly harvest. After five years, he recently got the property sold to another friend. I don't approve of his dealings with others on property matters. I don't even know if he has a count of the Power of attorney he holds. I can only worry at the end of the day!" he muttered and went on, "Anyways, Ranga, if you are under any pressure for funds, please insist on finding a buyer," said Ramanujam, more annoyed at his son.

What he had not revealed to Ranganathan were the moments of pride hearing the words of his colleague who had said, "*When I asked him how much I owe him for helping me with the sale, Amudan replied, "Nothing". When I insisted on paying, he asked if I could help with a recommendation for an Engineering college admission for a temple staff's son.*" Amudan's graciousness with money was not any surprise to Ramanujam but it was his pursuit of an "educational cause" that he felt was more gratifying if not redeeming!

The homestay project was, however, set in motion. It garnered mixed reactions from family members.

"*Anna*, be careful in your dealings with *Athimber*," warned Bhooma as Amudan was curling up on his cosy mattress on the terrace.

"What dealings?" asked Amudan.

"Don't involve yourself in his property matter. He is too money minded and I am afraid it will not end well. Plus, I think *Akka* must leave him soon."

She watched Amudan glower at her like he was going to explode.

"You don't know him, *Anna*. He is very different when he comes here. Acting like a gold-standard son-in-law. He doesn't treat *Akka* well. He yelled at her in front of me. He acts as if he is shouldering the whole world while all *Akka* does is sit pretty! I cannot digest this at all! She does everything for him, *Anna*. From handing him the first coffee to making sure his clothes were washed and ironed, cooking three delicious meals and all this apart from attending to Sarangan. But he does not seem to respect any of it. *Akka* is so nervous when he is around, especially when he comes back in a grumpy mood. You should see how she nervously waits on him while he eats! She keeps lamenting that he is too burdened at work and regrets not being able to help him much and says, "*Can't this Amudan lend him some help*!" My blood boils!!" She yawped.

"OK enough. I have to sleep," snapped Amudan, turning to the other side.

"I asked her to leave him soon," blurted Bhooma.

"How dare you!" sputtered Amudan as he sprang up in a rage.

"Well, who else will tell her!" she shrieked "Poor one, she used to be so laid back and happy at home here. She has completely changed now! Anxious and on her tows, 24/7 busy doing a thankless job!" She gasped, watching Amudan's face harden.

"I am being very patient, Bhooma!" he cautioned. "You have to stop now!"

"Of course, there is no use talking to you all. She is blind, deaf and drowned in love! No one can save her!" she bawled.

"*Anna*, I know two things for sure. One, I will never get married and second, I will never go and stay with them another time!"

The tears in her eyes as she left him with those words struck him harder.

Trade

"You are just like Padma!" His mother often told him. Amudan never could understand why. When it came to dedicating themselves blindly and unreservedly to something close to their hearts, they were alike. Only their object of surrender was different. For Padma, it was her husband, while for Amudan, it was *Lord Aravamudan*. They were steadfast in their paths.

"You should have thought about it before you asked the Minister to follow the queue," howled Kumaran. "This is his paternal property. He has finally inherited it and he can sell it to anyone who offers him the best price. ANYONE! We cannot stop him." He yelled at Amudan, who was quietly walking beside him. "He will not even entertain us, Amuda. What makes you think we can talk him out of it?"

Amudan was still quiet.

"Why are you coming in, Amuda? You wait outside. Let me alone go in. I will try to convince him." Kumaran implored as they stood outside the Minister's house.

They were made to wait for over a couple of hours and finally let in when the Minister seated on a reclining chair sized up Amudan, clad in a dhoti and a shirt and hollered for one of his men and instructed, "Bring...ONE chair."

"You sit, Amuda," said Kumaran.

Amudan stepping forward, pulled the chair and signalled for Kumaran to take the seat. Kumaran obeyed.

Kumaran slowly broached the topic, enquiring about the planned sale of the property and proposed, "I am interested in buying the property, Sir. You can quote your price."

The Minister let out a roar of laughter at it and said, "You cannot imagine, son! You cannot get anywhere near the quote. Anyway, the deal is closed. Go home and play!" He remarked vainly laughing at his own joke. "Is there anything else you want?" asked the Minister brusquely and added, "And why is this gentleman here? Does he need a donation or something?" He asked with a smirk of condescension.

"What do you want?" He prompted Amudan, who was mutely spectating.

Without batting an eyelid, Amudan spoke, "I want the respects offered by your family to Sarangapani *Perumal* to continue. We have seen your father offer his respects when our *Perumal* stood before your house during the processions. When you sell the property, sell it to someone who will continue the tradition," and paused, looking at the Minister, boring into his eyes.

"*Vaa Da*," muttered Amudan, casually patting Kumaran's shoulder while making his way out of the room.

The Minister sat aghast, watching him walk out. Amudan's words, loud and clear, still ringing in his ears, those daring eyes that looked right into his, left him with a shudder at every recall.

What was it? Was it the fear in his own heart or the fearlessness in Amudan's eyes?

"What was that, Amuda? Are you so naïve? Did you really think he cares about what you want? And why did you rush out of there?" asked Kumaran on their way back.

"I didn't rush. It was time to leave! We have said what we wanted to say," replied Amudan, looking away with Kumaran still staring at him in disbelief.

As they reached the temple, Amudan noticed that Malli had still not set up her flower shop. Without delving into it, he rushed to the altar of Lord Aravamudan to perform his daily service. As he stepped out a while later, he found Malli in her shop stringing flowers. Wrapping her *pallu* around her neck, her hair dishevelled, her face swollen and eyes brimming with tears; she went about her job.

"What happened? How did you get hurt?" asked Amudan, looking at her forehead bruised and swollen.

As she hesitantly looked up at him, he took a step back, seeing her bloodshot eyes full of tears.

"Malli, did someone hurt you? Who did this to you?" He questioned in shock. Embarrassed to even look up at him, Malli merely shook her head.

He hauled for a volunteer and said to Malli, "I will ask someone to string the flowers and mind the shop today.

You leave for the nursing home right now. I will send the collections to your home," he offered.

"I will manage," she replied. As Amudan turned to leave, "Can you buy me a glass of tea?" she asked. She cried her heart out while the volunteer had gone to get the tea. Amudan quietly stood watching until a friend of Malli came by.

When Amudan walked back inside the temple, he noticed a group of people huddled in a corner with Vasu *Bhattar* yelling at the top of his voice, "You should ask him, *Anna*. This should not go on. This kind of highhandedness should not be allowed. That flower vendor lady outside is crying. I know she was late. Find out what happened," threatened Vasu Bhattar.

Seeing Amudan walk towards them, Narayana Bhattar asked, "What happened to Malli, Amuda? Is anything wrong?" He enquired.

"Don't know what is wrong, but she is hurt," replied Amudan, as he looked around with concern.

"I will ask her, *Anna*. I will find out how she got hurt," said Vasu Bhattar and instantly hung his head down as Amudan shot him a glance. With more devotees coming in, Vasu Bhattar, still trembling from top to toe, walked back to the shrine.

A few days later, Amudan came to know that Vasu Bhattar had lodged a complaint with the temple Regulatory Board and the Local police station stating that Amudan was causing undue fear and mental agony to *Archakas* and all people serving at the temple with a request to oust him from the temple.

"Be careful, Amuda! You are making a lot of enemies," warned the Sub-Inspector of Police, a regular to the temple. "Do you want us to oust the *Archakar*, instead," joked a Temple Regulatory Board official after patiently reading out the entire complaint to Amudan. Neither of the complaints was entertained.

Though Amudan didn't speak a word about it to anyone, it did leave a thorn in his heart to learn that his presence was causing so much pain and discomfort to others. He was reminded of his father's words, "*There are definitely more people praying that Amudan stays out of the temple!*"

A strange feeling of shame and fear engulfed his mind as he walked into the temple that morning after his work in the fields. He trudged along the *Prakaram* with his head bent down and headed to the altar of Goddess Komalavalli. Like a mischievous child sneaking his way to his mother, fearing his father's wrath! He didn't have the courage to even step into the shrine of the Goddess. He stood outside watching Govindan perform the *Sahasranama Archana* in worship of the Goddess.

" Come, Amuda. Why are you standing outside?" asked Govindan as he finished the *Archana*.

"*Enna da*? You look too tired today, " observed Govindan, with a closer look at Amudan's ashen face, while he served the latter the *Theertha* prasadam.

As he softly pressed the *Shatari* on Amudan's head and held it for a little longer, he watched Amudan's body and lips quiver at the gesture. What was it?

Was it the gentle stroke of a mother's palm or the warmth of her loving embrace? How would you explain the magic of that healing touch? Or was it the "crown" of supreme solace that was rested on his head? The peace and relief it brought Amudan, were ineffable! Taking heart, he lifted his face to have a glimpse of the Goddess. He could do no more than that!

Noticing the beads of tears lining Amudan's eyes, Govindan asked, "Amuda, what is it? Please tell me. I have never seen you like this. Are you not well?" Amudan merely shook his head as he turned to leave. Govindan came rushing to stop him, gripping Amudan by his shoulders, "Wait! Did someone hurt you?" He uttered in shock, his voice turning feeble and shaking.

"Amuda, you slog on the fields every day so we can all peacefully enjoy our three meals. You will bear any amount of pain for our welfare. What is that even you cannot bear? What has brought you down today? What happened? Please talk to me." He prodded.

Amudan, with a dismissive nod, gruffly said, "Nothing," and sped his way out.

Vasu Bhattar, on the other hand, couldn't sleep through one night in peace! As much as he was in no doubt that Amudan's ways needed a lot of mending, he resented his own actions even more.

He worried if he had gone overboard in the matter, considering that everyone who had stood by him and fuelled his angst at Amudan refused to sign any petition before the Regulatory Board seeking action against Amudan.

The words of a senior *Archakar* echoed in his mind, "*You confront Amudan, warn him, thrash him as much as you wish, but don't turn the child in, please*!" He had begged. "*He may be right or wrong, but he is one among us, remember,*" another staff had warned.

Amudan was, after all, just about the age of a son he might have had. Perhaps he could have shown more restraint. But Amudan's impudence had offended him way too much, transgressing all his reserves of forbearance! The wounds Amudan's actions left in him were ingrained deep and remained fresh! For Vasu Bhattar ran over every painful event from the past to justify his actions! He could find reasons, but not any solace or his sleep!

It was Ranganayaki's words, though, that kept flashing in his mind. "*Who will tolerate the boy's attitude? We know that even our own children or spouses will not care to help us as Amudan does, but how can we put up with his temper outbursts? Everyone likes to have a cow in the house and milk it as much as they can. Who would like to clean up after it? Nuisance!*" She had casually commented.

Vasu Bhattar had only his conscience to convince. That was when he faintly hoped that no one would act upon his complaints!

While Amudan had not a moment left to revisit the incident. Like a child up in action after a fall, brushing away his bruises, Amudan went about his days with unmarred fervour and commitment.

The work on Ranganathan's property had fairly progressed. Retaining its vintage charm, the architecture, antique furniture, utensils and appliances were neatly done up and brought back to life. A magnificent swing made of recycled teak furniture at the centre of the house further enhanced its aesthetic appeal and a garden thoughtfully laid out in the backyard made it a complete home.

Even before the retiling of the floor and the interiors were completed, Amudan got the first booking for a week's stay for a friend's family settled abroad. Ranganathan and Padma were beyond thrilled!

Setting up their home with all the furniture and fittings for a comfortable stay of their guests, and reliving memories from every corner of the house, stoked up a sense of belongingness that they seemed to have forgotten these past years. More than anything, watching Sarangan run up and down the renovated house, proudly calling it "*My house!*" brimmed all their hearts full.

Developments

"*Anna, can you get me some Maruthani* leaves?" Sowmya had once asked Amudan. Her palms were hardly seen without the *mehendi* design ever since and a *Marudhani* bush now stood tall in Govindan's backyard.

Govindan, playing a friend, a father and a mother for Sowmya, did all that he could to help her feel at home. She persuaded him to teach Sanskrit lessons and deliver discourses on scriptures online. She lined up students from different time zones. She threw a fit if he slipped up even a bit. Smiling through his sleep-deprived eyes, Govindan embraced everything, every moment of his life as it came.

All their love and indulgences only left her more greedy and proud! She no longer even feigned any respect for Amudan. She was brutally demanding and brazenly curt in her dealings with him. Her attitude and tone made little difference to Amudan, but for Govindan, it was far too agonising to bear! His trust in the Gods he served though kept him going. Neither his endurance nor his trust was in vain!

One afternoon, around the closing time of the temple, Sowmya came rushing looking for Amudan. A lizard in the kitchen was tormenting her.

She slowed down, watching Govindan and Amudan walk out of the temple with Amudan helping the cleaner carry a heavy trash bin from the *Goshala*.

They were all shaken by the frail cry of Malli being roughed up by a man.

"*Dei*, leave her now!" bellowed Amudan as he charged towards the man who was holding Malli by her hair and loudly abusing her. The man was drunk and hearing Amudan's words, he began running, dragging Malli by her hair.

Watching Amudan pick up an iron rod in hand, Govindan ran towards him and held him back with all his might.

Amudan thrust himself forward shouting, "You let her go now or I will finish you today!" Fierce and out of control, everyone spectating, could see that Amudan meant those words.

As Amudan finally broke out of Govindan's hold, the drunken man swivelled to the ground and, dragging himself, he rushed on all fours, in fear for his life!

Sowmya stood aghast, watching Amudan. Wild and raging, he looked as implacable as a blazing missile in action. She shook as he zipped past her, his eyes still toasted with rage! There was no trace of the man that she had known him to be. She sullenly followed Govindan home, her hands cold and trembling.

Even the thought of Amudan only made her shudder every time. The dynamics changed!

As much as Amudan's anger was mostly validated, the extreme ferocity of its manifestation had anyone shocked and terrified. *It was his only protection, his inbuilt armour,* Kumaran and Desikan always reasoned.

Thaayaar and Perumal's protective veil around him, Govindan mused. It was his weapon as well, no doubt!

Malli carried on with her business as usual. Humiliating as her experiences were, she felt a tinge of relief now that there was nothing left to hide. She openly discussed her problems with the womenfolk of the town. Ranganayaki was her counsel mostly and, taking a special interest, suggested to Kumaran, "Kumara! Why don't you find a good job for our Malli's husband? He goes out of town on building contract work, it seems. It is the bad company at his workplace that is spoiling him, says Malli. Your friend will not understand all this. Who can even talk to him?" She muttered on.

Malli's husband, Murthy, was soon employed in Kumaran's factory. As much as he carried himself as a reformed man, he constantly felt under watch! Malli's life saw its first bloom- some respite! Her face lit up with a bright red *kumkuma* and her kohl-smeared eyes, her hair tied up into a neat bun, with a string of flowers tucked around it, Malli was seated in her flower shop, stringing flowers all day for the Lord and the Goddess.

It was a Sunday morning. After the *Pongal prasadam* distribution, Kumaran and Amudan retired to a quiet corner in the temple, a small passage couched between two walls. It was their favourite spot, where they spent hours, even as teenagers.

They sat by each other talking almost in whispers or just lost in their trails of thoughts. Today they were in deep contemplation as Kumaran was plotting ways to wriggle out of a proposal of love from his cousin with Amudan as his sounding board. His conscience, we could say.

"Is Amudan there?" They jolted, hearing Ramanujam's voice.

"Amuda, *Appa* has come," announced Kumaran, as he sprang up to his feet while Amudan further slid behind a pillar, blankly staring at Kumaran.

"Tell him a prospective groom and family are visiting us this evening to see Bhooma. They are expected to come by five o'clock. Ask him to stay at home," he said, throwing a furtive glance at Amudan.

As Kumaran turned to Amudan, the latter merely nodded, his eyes fixed on Kumaran.

The father and son were quite proficient in communicating in this manner for years now and had grown way more comfortable than others could imagine.

"Perundevi, I have informed your son about our visitors today. I cannot believe I found him in the same burrow he used to be hiding in as a schoolboy. Even the latest-born rats and cats in the temple must have moved many places by now. When will your son grow up?" mocked Ramanujam. Perundevi with a smile merely shook her head.

"I am serious! Now even Bhooma will move out of the house. What will he do?" asked Ramanujam. Perundevi knew better than to cross him in these times.

She quietly kept to her task of preparing savouries for the visitors that evening.

"One more thing, Ranganathan has told the groom's father that Amudan helps him in his business. Ask your son to be a little accommodating. Do you understand?

" Perundevi shot him a stern glance, and he quietly wiggled away.

How unfortunate! She thought. *Like a person who owned a chest of diamonds, thinking they were all just some shiny pebbles.* Ramanujam's only grouse was that his son was not like everybody else. In his haste to compare with others, he hardly noticed what his son was really made of!

Perundevi wished someone could notice her son! "*The glint in his eyes, his nimble hands at work! Whether he held a chisel, shovel or sickle, his dexterous manoeuvres were hard not to notice! Sunshine or rain, he never missed a day on the field. Bustling through the day, with a million things he did, he would skip a meal, but never turn down a call for help! Anyone, anytime!*"

"*Could no one see the copiousness of his heart in all that? In his silence, in his toil or in all his loud exhortations, could they not find any trace of the love he bore so deep? Could they not stop to watch the unwearied glow on his face, no matter what life may throw at him? The sublimity of his contentment- can all the currency in the world ever stand a price to that? Indeed, there cannot be another like my Amudan!*" she thought, her heart swelling with pride.

"*Amma,*" she heard Amudan calling as he rustled into the house.

"Where is the groom's party coming from? Does Bhooma know? Is she ready… for marriage?" he inquired while washing his hands and legs.

Perundevi looked at him long and hard.

"Who cares about all that? The family is known to your *Athimber*. He thinks it will be a suitable alliance for Bhooma. Since they would be here to visit the temple, he suggested that they meet us. "

He quietly squeezed the batter into the oil and smiled at his mother, watching a flowery *Jangiri* spin and sizzle in the oil pond.

He rarely smiled, but when he did, his eyes dazzled like a pristine pair of diamonds, his innocent face buzzing with the joy of a three-year-old.

"Perundevi" they heard Ramanujam's voice and their smiles vanished.

"I will have to check on Bhooma," she muttered as she rose to leave, pressing her hands on Amudan's shoulders.

"*Anna*, tell *Appa* that I am not interested in this alliance," whispered Bhooma quietly munching on a *Bonda* freshly out of the pan, clad in a beautiful *Kancheepuram* silk saree, hair neatly braided, the string of fresh jasmine flowers, tucked over the braid.

"Why? You don't quite look like you are not interested," he said with a teasing smile, looking into her eyes perfectly lined with kajal.

"I am serious. I don't want to be rushed this way! Please stop this," she said and scooted back to her room, gobbling up another *Bonda*.

The groom's party finally arrived. All through the introductions and pleasantries, Bhooma stood around with a listless expression while Amudan served the snacks and coffee for the guests.

With the groom's father taking a special interest in Amudan, ever since he mentioned *"I mostly work at the temple!"*, when asked about his job, the rest of the discussions were centred around the temple and its customs.

While Amudan enthusiastically shared every trivia about the temple and the town, to an engrossed audience, Ramanujam sat with his head hung down and Bhooma with an unmissable frown!

The Unexpected

Later that night, Amudan was returning home after the *Sayana Arthi* at the temple.

Puffing and gasping, Bhooma came running behind and asked, "Did you tell Appa?"

"Tell what? You tell him whatever you have to say. Tell Athimber, in fact," replied Amudan.

"Why should I tell *Athimber*? He never asked my permission before he invited these people," retorted Bhooma.

With a disapproving glance at her, Amudan quietly walked on.

"Did you hear the boy's mother when she said, "*My son does not know how to cook, so we have asked him to get married and leave for the States*?" Is that why I was born and raised for, *Anna*? To cook and serve someone I never knew to this day existed? "

"*Anna*, please understand. I don't want a life like *Amma*'s or *Akka*'s, spending my days entirely in the kitchen and tending to family and children. I have dreams beyond that. No one else will understand what I mean."

"I don't understand either. What do you want to do?" snapped Amudan.

"Don't talk to me this way, *Anna*!" she bleated and led Amudan by his hand to a *thinnai* of a locked house.

"Who else can I talk to? I want to marry someone who will treat me as an equal.

Someone who can respect my choice to pursue a career. Someone who will be an equal partner at home in every way."

With exasperation, Amudan said, "Where will they go hunting for your equal partner, Bhooma? How would we know? Or how do you know this poor gentleman who came today, will not turn out to be one? "

"*Anna*, one more thing. My marriage has to be entirely your responsibility. I don't want *Athimber* to interfere in this. I don't trust him with this."

"Outrageous! You are being very unreasonable, Bhooma! He means well and looks out for you as a brother!"

"He need not!" She cut in. "When I have a brother! You don't shirk me off! Promise me you will take complete charge of my marriage! *Appa* or *Athimber,* should not spend a penny on my wedding! I don't want to entertain their patriarchal ego with my marriage."

"Then you better fend for yourself," retorted Amudan. "Why do you need me? I don't have a penny, anyway! We will all step back!" He paused and went on.

"Bhooma, if you are not interested in this alliance, just say that much. Just plainly say that to *Appa* or I will say that to *Athimber*, if you want. But don't you dare say a word more!" He uttered in a firm, threatening tone. She jumped out of the *thinnai* and whisked away in a fury.

He sat on ruminating over her words. For someone whose mind was never used to treading on people, their outlook or emotions, empathising with Bhooma has never been easy.

For the amount of time she spent speculating over people's motives and her responses while in constant fear of being exploited, Amudan would rather be cheated and get done with it! Many times over!

However, it is not to say that Amudan was above emotions. His emotions, anger, anxiety and desire, if at all, were only more intense but were all parked elsewhere. He was never at the centre of them!

Roaring and hissing, for the imposing personality that he came across as, who would imagine how quiet and immaculate his mind really was? As much as his inscrutable countenance gave very little away, who would fail to notice his eyes bustling with life and vitality?

Wide-eyed and bursting with energy is how he woke up and went about each day. There was no dearth of challenges in his life, but ticking like a clock, the zest, assiduity and fortitude he could muster even in the gravest of situations- was far beyond reckoning! What drove him? What gave him strength? What was his vision, his quest? What were his vigilant eyes always on the lookout for?

Anything and everything around him that he noticed, good or bad, like a magnet to the north pole, his mind would lead to Lord *Aravamudan* and the Goddess. His ardour or agitation was all based around the deities as well. If all the love we feel for a living being is on account of the divinity of the soul that dwells in them, what can we say of the love for the divine forms themselves? Amudan's heart only grew fonder by the day!

The serenity and the unbridled happiness he felt, we can only wish to perceive! But where did it all begin for Amudan?

Like any child raised in a temple town, Amudan's visits to the temple couched on his mother's hip, were regular. This child was different though. Amudan refused to eat unless he was fed in the vicinity of the temple. Everyone in the town knew he loved to play in the little yard before the shrine of Goddess Komalavalli.

It was a delight to watch the child point his little fingers to the shrine of Goddess Komalavalli, saying, "*Amma,*" as he was taught by his mother! She fed him in the temple yard, telling him the story of Ramayana, not as happenings of a distant century in the past but as the story of the presiding deities of the temple.

When speaking of Lord Rama and Goddess Sita she always referred to them as *Amudan Ummachi* and *Amma Ummachi*. For the first time when he heard the part of the abduction of Sita, Amudan's eyes welled with tears, his lips quivering, and he began to weep inconsolably. Perundevi rushed the child to the shrine to pacify him and showed him Goddess Komalavalli, saying that Ravana left *Amma Ummachi* behind because little Amudan was crying. That was the only version of Ramayana he could stomach. As every time Perundevi tried to progress beyond, Amudan would stop her short, saying "*Amma! Amma!*" pointing to the shrine. He stood guard to the Goddess ever since.

Amudan was now twenty-four years of age. He did not fear a *Ravana* anymore.

However, every person who showed the slightest disrespect to the deities, the temple premises or rules, was the one he stood guard against, with every ounce of his being. Every event, activity and person connected to the temple was his business. The four streets around the temple were the kingdom he guarded. Nothing went unnoticed by him, he had a count of even the stray dogs in those streets. Had ways of connecting with them, no leash, no name, but a special bond without attachments of any kind!

It was two days since the conversation with Bhooma. With Amudan's preoccupation with the temple affairs, the event rarely crossed his mind.

Bhooma mostly kept to herself, her mind raging every time at the sight of Amudan or her father. She had told her mother she needed some time to think before deciding on the alliance. She refused to answer the calls from her sister.

It was a regular morning at the temple. Devotees lining up in the queue for darshan. Preparations were underway for the *Thirumanjanam* of the deities. Amudan was supervising the cleaning and arrangements for the event when they were all jolted by a loud wail from the *Nandavanam*.

Amudan rushed towards the *Nandavanam* and halted at the entrance, watching Komala and her friends swarming out, in a panic. "What?" He enquired, looking at them, perplexed.

"A snake, Amuda!" replied Komala, horrified. "A huge one!" She spoke between gasps, hardly able to hold her breath and turning back she shouted,

"Come, Bhooma!" Shocked to see Bhooma standing like a statue staring at the ground.

Amudan forged in towards Bhooma and watched the snake before her, its hood lifted. He stepped in between and in a soft voice said, "Bhooma, come this way! It wouldn't harm you."

Watching her still look frozen in fear, he took a step behind, closer to the snake. Bhooma, in shock, looked up at him when he gently led her away to the entrance, where Komala was still waiting anxiously. Bhooma was still in a trance as she walked beside Komala, who held her tight and slowly walked her towards the shrine of Goddess *Andal*.

The incident left many in shock and, most of all, Bhooma. She was withdrawn and in a deep, pensive state ever since. Her mother and Komala were her only comfort.

Amudan, after the evening pooja, noticed Desikan's mother walking out of the shrine of the Goddess. He walked towards her enquiring, "How is *Mama*? He couldn't come today?" and placed a generous portion of the *prasadam* in her hands.

"He has still not finished his daily *parayanam,*" she replied.

"Amuda, can you come home sometime? *Mama* seems a bit upset. He is not talking to anyone. He did not even want to come to the temple today. He might talk to you. Can you come?" She asked, looking at him expectantly.

He nodded and, much to her joy, he quietly walked along with her as she left the temple later.

Desikan's parents were among the people Amudan cared for most. They were a family who served the temple for almost two generations. Desikan's father, Narasimhachar, a retired Sanskrit professor, an exponent of the Vedic scriptures and an ardent follower of *Sri Vaishnava sampradaya*, led a pious life, committing himself to the reading of the scriptures, rendering discourses on them and teaching the same.

To Amudan, he was like one of the pillars of this temple. His very presence was a lot of strength. Although Amudan never got around to attending any of his classes or discourses, he still cherished their bond, silent but strong.

Desikan's parents were among the few who respected Amudan for who he was. Having watched him through his growing years, they had learnt to look beyond his curt manners and never refrained from expressing their appreciation for his quiet ways of helping everyone. They knew they could trust him as their own son, if not more!

"Is it Amudan?" chirped Narasimhachar. "Come! Come! How are you?" He enquired, as Amudan nodded in affirmation.

"You couldn't come today?" asked Amudan, as plainly as a five-year-old. Desikan's mother, Vedavalli, hastened to hand the *prasadam* to her husband, saying, "See how generously Amudan has given us *prasadam*. He walked all the way home with me, asking for you. "

"Indeed, Amudan's generosity can only be matched by *Perumal* himself!" He replied with a soft smile at Amudan, which was not quite reciprocated. Typically!

"Amuda, how is your father? I think of him a lot these days," remarked Narasimhachar.

"We are different personalities altogether, your father and me. We both share a similar fate, though! We may be respected by people around us, but not by our own sons. That's our curse, perhaps. We can only wish well for everyone, isn't it? " he went on.

"Amuda, remember one thing. Your father, even if you hurt him all his life, will only wish the best for you," he said as he choked on his words.

Amudan was more perplexed now!

"To see my son married and settled is what I want. Is that asking too much? My son has asked me not to look for a bride for him," he added, Desikan's words ringing loud in his ears, "*Why do you want me to get married? What do you know about me to find a suitable person for me? Do you even know what I like and what I don't?*" He is right. I might not know what he likes and what he does not, but I certainly know what is good for him," went on the senior man.

"An astrologer had predicted many years back that Desikan's marriage should be conducted in a temple for it to last. I took his words with a silent vow to get Desikan married at our temple premises when it happens. I have kept this to myself all these years. Only our *Perumal* knows about this. He is also quiet now." He mumbled, with tears brimming in his eyes.

"I am sorry, Amuda. I have bored you with my worries. I feel very fragile these days. I am old and tired and easily emotional," he reasoned as if he were talking to himself.

"That is why I am scared to even meet people. I prefer to stay at home. You can come anytime to see me." He said, looking up at Amudan with a smile.

Amudan sat beside him for a while more, giving all the comfort a quiet company can offer and took leave with the words, "Will see you at the temple, *Mama*!"

It was a day after the incident at the *Nandavanam*. Amudan had left strict instructions to leave the gate of the *Nandavanam* closed.

Komala walked in with a few of her friends, still haunted by the incident the day before. It was her daily duty to string the garlands for the deities, along with her friends while they sang the hymns of the *Azhwars*. The time she most looked forward to every day.

Today, as the flower brigade arrived, they all were astonished to see the flowers were already gathered, neatly sorted and stacked, ready to be strung into garlands. From the sheer orderliness of it, Komala could sense Amudan's hand in it. She heaved a deep sigh.

Respite

"Govinda, I will be going to the bazaar. Do you need anything?" asked Amudan.

"Sure, some peace of mind!" replied Govindan, gritting his teeth as he locked the door of *Thaayaar Sannidhi*. His phone was constantly ringing.

Kumaran, with a sardonic smile at Amudan, said, "If an *Archakar* serving the Goddess cannot find peace of mind, where can you and I find it, Amuda?"

"You haven't lost it still, let me remind you!" quipped Govindan. "Enjoy it while it lasts." He mumbled on.

His phone still kept ringing.

"Why don't you answer the phone?" Amudan snapped.

"I don't have answers, that's why!" retorted Govindan as Kumaran broke into a chuckle.

"Don't laugh, Kumara! It's serious. Sometimes I just want to give up."

"What do you mean?" quizzed Amudan.

"She is used to a lot of comforts that I hardly know of, and I am not able to provide her with any of that. I don't like to take anything from her father as well. She torments me now, saying we should move out of town and that I should earn more money. I don't know what *Thaayaar* and *Perumal* have in mind for me. I don't know how long I can serve them here."

"Stop that, Govinda! You will go nowhere. Just tell her you cannot! How can you even think of such a proposition? What does she want, anyway?" Amudan asked.

"That's a long list! Air conditioner, washing machine, computer.. there's more!" He listed.

"What?" squawked Amudan. "Where will he go for all that?" He whined in shock, turning to Kumaran.

"Just tell her you cannot afford any of that! Make it very clear," he added while Govindan's face hardened.

Govindan shook his head with exasperation, saying, "You cannot understand, Amuda. Just leave it. "

Morose and withdrawn was how Govindan was seen, mostly. A sight Amudan helplessly bore with!

Bhooma ever since her conversation with Amudan felt lost. With Amudan, the only one she trusted always, not giving her much hope, she almost resigned to her fate. She didn't have the courage to fight any more. Amudan's resounding words, "*You better fend for yourself*" kept ringing in her ears. Amudan had always looked out for her all along. Every little thing he ensured would go as she wished, even without her asking for it. How could he let her down on such a crucial life decision as this? Ask her to fend for herself? She knew he was angry at her. She knew he never liked her to speak disrespectfully about her father or brother-in-law. She still had to speak her mind. She believed beyond all this that he would never fail her. She blindly trusted him, as always, even now.

"Has Bhooma eaten?" asked Amudan as Perundevi laid the plantain leaves for lunch.

"Not yet. She is still upset, Amuda. Call her, she must be in the backyard, "replied Perundevi.

Amudan peeped out and found her washing her clothes. Seeing her not respond to his call, he walked over and stood before her.

"What?" she demanded, gloomily staring at him.

"You tell me. What is bothering you?" enquired Amudan.

"You don't know?" she asked.

He shook his head and said," I am not sure."

"What is it? Is it about the alliance or the snake?" He asked.

"Was it a poisonous one, *Anna*? It could have killed me, right? Was it angry at me?"

"No. She was scared of you, that's all," he replied.

"I don't know what to make of all this, *Anna*. I am very scared to decide on anything. I don't know what would have happened to me that day if you hadn't come. What if you had been in the fields? Left at its mercy in those moments, it was the truth staring at me that I cannot control many things in life." She recalled pensively.

Watching him look at her with concern, she went on.

"About the alliance, there is nothing to think about. I have told you all that I needed to say. I don't need any ornaments or silk drapes. Just a cotton saree, the sacred thread and a simple wedding will do, but I want only you to spend every penny for my wedding."

"You may have forgotten, *Anna*, but this is a vow I took long back with all the family around. I will stand by it and I want to marry only a man who will respect this. I am left at your mercy, though. You decide whether to stand up for me or not."

"What! That was no vow, Bhooma. Just an angry statement you made on an impulse. That is all. We have all moved on. Stop making a fool of yourself now," advised Amudan.

"It was not a statement out of impulse, *Anna*! It was a vow I took wholeheartedly. I know that as much as our *Perumal*, you and I hold in our hearts. I don't have to prove its sanctity to anyone else," she said and indignantly sat down on the washing stone, staring back at him.

"Bhooma, you are complicating your life. As you rightly said, these things you are asking for are not entirely in our control. I understand your pride was hurt then, but we cannot make our lives about it! I will even understand if you tell me that you don't wish to be married at all! Or that you have someone in mind whom you wish to marry and I will stand by you. But this.."

"I wish to marry Desikan," the words almost tumbled out of her mouth. Amudan looked up at her with a jolt.

She instantly covered her face with her palms, more shocked by her statement. She missed watching the glint of joy in her brother's eyes as he heaved a deep sigh of relief.

Amudan quietly sat beside her and began dialling a number on his phone.

"Desika, can we talk?" asked Amudan to the caller on the phone with Bhooma looking at him with the wonder of a child.

"Of course. Any time! I am surprised I crossed your mind at this hour," replied Desikan with a chortle.

"Would you like to marry Bhooma?" asked Amudan as Bhooma once again covered her face with her palms. Amudan broke into a wide grin, watching her.

There was silence at the other end of the call.

"Desika, would you like to marry my sister, Bhooma?" Amudan asked again as Bhooma, choking with emotions, quietly leaned on his shoulder.

"Amuda, are you serious? Or am I dreaming?" uttered Desikan, barely gathering his words.

"I have been meaning to speak to you about this for so long. I cannot believe you brought it up now. I have always liked Bhooma. Not sure she knew it. Never dared to speak to her or you about it. What can I say, Amuda? Will Bhooma like me?"

Amudan breathed out a chuckle at that.

"We had a family visit us a few days back. An alliance for Bhooma. She was not keen to pursue it," he said and paused.

"Well, *Appa* does not know about this. I will broach it with him, and then you can talk to your parents."

"Amuda, you have no idea how this feels to me. I can hardly believe my ears. Thank you, *Da*."

"Not as yet. Let's wait till we have my father's approval on this. You know him. Now that I am in the picture you should know this is not going to be easy."

"Coming to think of it, can you talk to *Appa* instead," asked Amudan. "Don't even bring this conversation to his knowledge. Things might move faster, isn't it?" Amudan thought aloud.

"No, Amuda. I want you to initiate it. However difficult it may be or however long it might take, I want you to get us married. There is no other way I would want it."

" Speaking of which, it will be a very simple wedding, my friend. Bhooma wants me to entirely bear the wedding expenses. So, it will probably be a wedding in the temple with *Perumal Chakarapongal, Puliyodare and Dhadhyonnam* for all invitees and devotees. She will walk home with you right after that. I hope that will do."

"Bhooma alone will do for me!" replied Desikan, still struggling to believe his ears.

This was indeed all that she wanted! Amudan was convinced as well.

Over lunch, Amudan and Bhooma filled in their mother with the developments. She was overjoyed to watch Bhooma chirpy as ever.

Taking on Ramanujam was, however, no mean task.

"*Appa*, Desikan and Bhooma like each other. Desikan said he will speak to his father to take things forward," mentioned Amudan as he watched a storm of rage wash over his father.

"How will I tell Ranganathan about this? How can we embarrass him this way? What about the family that visited us? Do you people even have an idea of their standing in society? Do you even care? Where was Desikan all this while? Why didn't she tell us earlier?"

It took a different turn when Perundevi pitched in, saying, "We never spoke to Bhooma about her marriage. How would she tell us? The child had kept it to herself, all the while scared about our reaction until she opened up to Amudan." She then pacified him, saying, "Let Amudan deal with this. You have always wanted him to take responsibility. Let us not discourage him now."

With a lot that needed to be said being spoken, the house fell silent for a long time.

While Perundevi and Kumaran were quietly taking stock of and assimilating Amudan's savings and investments for Bhooma's wedding, with an unexpected commission that Amudan was paid for a property deal, Govindan's quaint little house got crowded with an Air conditioner, a Computer and a Washing Machine.

Kumaran and Perundevi were left immensely shocked and upset.

"How will I answer Appa?" she asked, masking a million more questions in her mind. "Why didn't you consult with me?" Kumaran asked.

"That money came for Govindan. Just in time. He needs it now," was all the reply they got. *Did Bhooma even cross his mind?* Neither of them dared to ask.

Any more discussion on this matter with Amudan they knew would be futile!

His priorities in life or ways with money were quite difficult to fathom, let alone digest. Amudan, though, realised he had ruffled more feathers now. He wasn't worried about Bhooma's wedding one bit. From his own experiences, he knew money would eventually make its way, if and when he needed it. That was the time value of money, as he saw!

In his holistic outlook, one's efforts and rewards belonged to all, while money was just a medium that kept moving, always finding its purpose on the way. He only cared enough to park it to where it was most needed and just in time!

Govindan continuing to serve at the temple was to Amudan, any day, a purpose beyond a price! Amudan hoped this would bring some relief to Govindan, at least.

Alas, little did he know it was the gluttony of desire that he was feeding and that Govindan was still being preyed upon. Only more humbled and indebted now, Govindan quietly bore the taunts, determined to keep Amudan out of it from then on. While Sowmya hardened even more, her discomfort around Amudan now taking fresh shoots. She lived her days with a silent resolve to not bear a child until they moved out of the town!

A few weeks passed. It was days of torture for Bhooma with her father not looking her in the eye or speaking to her. Being the little one of the family, she had only enjoyed all their warmth and affection all this while.

Her father would be harsh on Padma and Amudan but had never raised his voice at her, although she was the naughtiest of the lot. His cold disposition to her now was shocking and draining her.

Amudan was leaving for his usual field visit when he saw Bhooma hand their father coffee in a tumbler.

Ramanujam, with a look of disgust, turned away from her. Amudan watched her stand there trembling with the tumbler in hand, her fear-laden eyes helplessly reaching for him.

"Don't do this, Appa," blurted Amudan, unable to take the sight. Ramanujam looked up at him in disbelief.

"Don't be cold to her! What is that you want?" Amudan went on. "She will not marry anyone against your wish. You know that! She has only expressed her wish, nothing more."

"Scold her, as much as you have to, but don't put her through this, please! She cannot bear it," uttered Amudan, taking a deep breath.

"She is not used to it," he said as Bhooma left the tumbler on the table and rushed into her room, whimpering.

Ramanujam's eyes softened upon hearing those words. He kept looking at Amudan like he was seeing him for the first time. He looked at those eyes, glistening and red with emotions. It tore his heart to see the pain they bore. It had been years since he called his son "Amuda!", addressed him directly or even cared to look at him as he spoke. He watched Amudan turn and leave. His mind went back years behind, and as far as he could reach, he couldn't recall the last time he had seen Amudan smile at him.

He shut his eyes in despair, gulping a heavy lump in his throat. A huge wave of emotions swamped his heart!

It was the month of *Chithirai*. While the town was preparing for the ten-day annual festival, the Minister's house was full of activity, men and women, all over, busy cleaning and decorating with festoons of lights and plantain trees, rumours abuzz in the town. The word got around that the entire family had come down to witness the temple festivities.

With more party vans and media beginning to swarm the town, Amudan and the team spent endless hours closely coordinating with the police patrol for crowd management and parking arrangements.

Putting to rest all speculations, the latest bulletin from Ranganayaki's *thinnai* revealed that the Minister's daughter-in-law in London had conceived after fifteen years of marriage and as a mark of their respect and gratitude, the family wanted to resume their *Mandagapadi* for Lord Sarangapani after a hiatus of almost a decade.

That evening, the procession of Sarangapani *Perumal,* halted before the Minister's house. The Minister, clad in a dhoti and an *Angavastram* respectfully wrapped around his waist, stood bearing a *Purnakumbam* in hand, surrounded by his family members, welcoming the Lord and his consorts with offerings of baskets of fruits and flowers. Amudan and Kumaran, standing in the front, among the palanquin bearers, exchanged a quiet glance.

Pot of Gold

Bhooma and Desikan's wedding dates were finally fixed. Desikan's parents were delighted beyond words.

With a huge burden lifted off his chest, Narasimhachar, overwhelmed with awe and gratitude, said to his wife, "Never take our Amudan for granted! He walked in casually the other day and just lent me his ear as I poured my heart out to him! When he left our house, I felt an inexplicable relief at having done my part. It was the moment I realised that it was not "my burden" to bear!" He broke into tears at that. "Our *Perumal* took away even the one last wish I was attached to all along and showed me the path of absolute surrender. He had sent that child to me for that. To the world, Amudan maybe anyone, but to me, he is my guide, my *Acharyan*!" He declared with folded hands.

With Padma and Ranganathan unreservedly celebrating the news of Bhooma and Desikan's wedding and Amudan's fervent involvement in it, Ramanujam felt quite relieved. Bhooma's wedding was indeed the buzz of the town and with the news of Amudan conducting it, making the rounds, every friend and contact of Amudan poured in their support in currency and kind. Perundevi and Kumaran could barely track the source to even thank them.

A five-day wedding was planned with all the rituals in place and the main event was conducted on the temple premises, as wished by Desikan's father, which was followed by an elaborate wedding lunch for family, friends and the people of the town.

The wedding functions were all over, and it was the day Bhooma and Desikan were to leave for Delhi, accompanied by Padma and Ranganathan.

Bhooma was busy packing her suitcase. She noticed a beautiful quilt woven out of the softest of her mother's cotton sarees. She immediately rushed out of the room, looking for Amudan. Hoping to find him in the temple, she came out running, not realising it was way past the temple closing time.

Finding the house still crowded, Amudan and Desikan had chosen a deserted *thinnai,* to spend some quiet time with each other. Hearing a voice calling out, "Bhooma, why are you running like this?", Amudan peeped out.

She halted on seeing the two men and sprinted over to them. Still panting, she stood staring at Amudan with a faint smile.

"You have given me everything I asked for. You have not even spared a scrap of cloth that I had ever wished. I cannot go away leaving you alone," she said, batting her tear-filled eyes.

Removing the gold chain from her neck that she had treasured all these years, she put it around Amudan's neck, saying," Don't ever remove this!"

Not waiting for a moment more, she scooted back to their home, wiping her eyes. Amudan and Desikan sat watching her run all the way back until she disappeared into the house.

"She cannot wash her clothes. She cannot cook a thing. She can read and talk all day," declared Amudan with a scoff, turning to look at Desikan.

"She wants to pursue a law degree," replied Desikan with a smile.

"Very well then," muttered Amudan with relief.

Yet another bright morning and the Sun God in all his glory was warming up to a scorching day. Amudan was still in the field with the farmers when they heard the noise of a motorbike, halted and throttling. It was about time for him to leave for the temple.

"Amuda!" The funds are still pouring in, "exclaimed Kumaran as Amudan was cleaning his muddied hands and feet.

"What funds?" he asked, drying his hands.

"The funds for Bhooma's wedding," replied Kumaran.

"What! Send it all back to them. Whatever is left. Ask them to stop sending the funds," Amudan snapped with a frown as he hopped onto the rear seat of the bike.

As Kumaran wrote back to the group of friends with an account of the wedding expenses and the amount remaining unspent, it was unanimously decided that the same must be kept aside as "Amudan Fund" for all the future development activities that he wished to carry out in the temple or town.

When Kumaran responded by saying, "Will check with Amudan if he is ok with it," one friend replied, "Why don't you buy him a smartphone at least now?"

"Oh, I have tried! "he replied, "They don't fit well into the fold of his *angavastram,* he claims."

"Amudan *Goshti* Trust" was set up with Kumaran and Perundevi as its trustees, to fund any temple repairs, maintenance or festival spending and towards financial support for *Archakas*, educational support, seed funding or medical support to anyone and everyone in the town who needed help.

It was strange how in the small town where every word got around, it was only one side of the story that people chose to believe. That Amudan was now a rich man, sitting on a hefty sum of money and acres of fields under his watch.

Every act of his was seen through a prism of doubt and deceit.

"Amudan has the choicest blessing of Mahalakshmi, Komalavalli *Thaayaar,*" remarked Ranganayaki's friend as she was helping the latter draw the pastes of *elai vadam* to dry. "You must agree, Bhooma's was among the grandest weddings. Perundevi, after all these years, is finally beaming with pride. Two daughters married and Amudan doing well for himself, what more would the parents want to see?" she innocuously mentioned.

"Doing well? What do you mean by that? All this is Kumaran's work, I tell you. Amudan wouldn't know a thing!" roared Ranganayaki.

"It's nothing new for a wedding to be conducted out of gifts from friends and relatives. Bhooma's wedding was just one like that. I am quite sure Amudan didn't ask for any of it, though he deserved all the support he got and more. The poor boy has no proper education or a job, nor does he know the worth of the money he has now! Would he have given it away for charity had he known?" she muttered.

"So, what has changed for Amudan now? Nothing. Even long after you and I have been gone and all our children have moved countries, Amudan will remain in the town cleaning the temple and cutting the grass. Why, Amudan was here even last night. He changed the tiles in our backyard overnight when he heard that my husband tripped and almost fell!" She added with a smirk.

"You tell me, Parimala, which girl of this day and age will come forward to marry a man like him? Why, now that you think he is doing well, will you give your daughter in marriage to him?" challenged Ranganayaki candidly.

Perundevi's heart swelled with pride every time to think of the many people who were by Amudan's side, who understood his true worth. No richest stud of diamonds could have pleased her ears more than the words of gratitude of people as they heartily praised her son, acknowledging all that he had done for them. She was not the one to be cowed down by rumours and taunts.

She only looked at them as the vain attempts of those who, blinded by his sheer glow, couldn't bear to see him shine! Perundevi could stomach it all, but not these utterances of Ranganayaki!

Although she had known Ranganayaki for years and was aware of all her uncharitable comments about every family member of hers, including Amudan, she had dismissed them all, thinking, *"It's a curse to have a tongue like hers!"*

Ranganayaki's words this time went piercing right through her heart! It shattered in a moment all the joyous memories of the past. Perundevi stood like a stone, too shocked, too pained as she heard a friend recount Ranganayaki's words over a phone call.

Amudan had left for the fields, Ramanujam was getting ready to leave for a wedding and Perundevi could barely move a limb. She sank to the floor and quietly lay down, excusing herself from the wedding event. Once Ramanujam left, shutting the door behind him, she sobbed her heart out within the closed walls of the house.

Every mother would only pray and wish to raise a virtuous child, not a genius nor a rich one! Amudan is more than I could ever have wished for, but now, can I not wish to see him happily married? Can I not wish for all the joys of a family life for him?

Will he be shunned away by all? For what reason? That he chose a life different from the rest? Even thieves, murderers, conmen, even the lame and perverted have families and children, but my blemishless son has no place here? Thoughts kept rushing in until a pang of guilt left her choking.

Have I driven Amudan to this? I put in all my strength to fight for whatever he wanted, instead, should I have forced Amudan out of the town, and into the real world? Was it in my control at all? Perumal and Thaayaar are the only world he knows! She began sobbing helplessly at that.

Unable to reign in her mind that went spiralling down a vicious thread, she meekly followed it until she dozed off.

Perundevi woke up with a jolt to the sound of the temple bells and almost instantly slumped back to the floor with a pounding headache. It was the *"Uchikaala"* puja around noon in the temple when food was offered to the deities. She had not cooked anything for lunch yet. She knew Amudan would walk in anytime soon, hungry after the day's toil. As she struggled to rise and sit up, she checked herself as she thought, "*Just as for anybody else in the town, was he just a son born to slog and serve, for Perumal and Thaayaar as well? Would they even care enough if the child starved?*" She shut her eyes, unable to bear the thought.

She heard the gate clink open. She could hear Amudan's quick steps. She rose to sit up as the door was thrust open. She looked up at Amudan, with all her guilt, pain and fear gripping harder.

"What happened?" mumbled Amudan, shocked to see the state she was in, dishevelled and panic-stricken. He had no memory of seeing his mother that way. "You didn't go to the wedding?" he inquired.

Perundevi was still dazed and staring at the large bundle of dry *Mantharai* leaf in Amudan's hand.

"Rama *Bhattar* handed the *prasadam* to me on my way back from the temple," he said, pointing to the bundle in his hand. "He asked me to take it home since they were all heading for the wedding lunch, "detailed Amudan.

It was quite unusual for Amudan to carry so much of the *prasadam* home. He would usually find someone on the way and distribute it.

Watching Perundevi still look at him bemused, he asked, "Are you not well? Should we go to the doctor?"

Perundevi cut in saying, "I am very hungry, Amuda," and stretched her palm out, her weary eyes imploring him.

Amudan rushed to clean himself up and sat with his mother, patiently handing her the *prasadam* as she took one mouthful at a time, watching her sob, sniffle, and gasp like a child between bites.

No questions, no words of comfort, no look of concern, he quietly nourished her as he would, a withered plant.

Whether it was just eating out of her son's hand, or the ethereal energy from the food she consumed, she felt an overwhelming relief.

It was the comfort of her silent cries being heard! The calming respite of being eased of the deepest fears, worries and doubts bottled up in her that had held her captive for years. The soul-soothing solace of being reassured that her faith, her path and her struggle haven't been in vain.

She felt like a child herself pacified, tucked, and tended in a protective fold, just when she needed it!

Immersed in the warmth of that moment, her mind almost barren of thoughts, she sat, savouring the taste of a sublime sweetness. The nectar called Grace!

A perilous state

"Amudan's economics is quite baffling," as Ranganathan put it, referring to all the activities Amudan was funding while still working in the temple, the fields and the neighbourhood homes, clad in a simple white dhoti and shawl.

There were conspiracy theories of Kumaran and his father siphoning money and setting up Amudan. They were waiting for the bubble to burst! Komala was among those who thought he was being set up. There was an ominous fear deep down of something terrible about to ensue! She couldn't discuss it with anyone. Her chants of *Sudarshana Ashtakam* doubled, with the prayer to keep all evil at bay.

Rumours were mounting, some wrote to the Temple Regulatory Authority, of a suspicion of corruption at the temple and funds being siphoned. Kumaran's father, with his links at the helm, quietened the noise in a go.

It was a Friday afternoon, about the temple closing time. Manikandan and Vasu *Bhattar* were the last ones to leave the temple, and the main entrance door was being drawn shut. Amudan waiting outside settling accounts with the flower vendor called out, "Manikanda, are you sure there is no one inside? Did you check? Check once again," he said.

Being used to keeping a watch on the persons who entered and exited the temple, he couldn't recall noticing a particular gentleman exit.

When Manikandan returned saying there was no one inside, Amudan, growing anxious, walked into the temple, whispering to Manikandan, "Lock the door and wait outside till I call you."

He sneaked inside the temple and hid behind the wall adjacent to the entrance gate and waited. A few minutes later, he heard a faint rustle of footsteps from inside. Amudan sprinted to the other side and looked from behind the wall opening into the outer passage of the temple. He could see the man emerge from behind the passage of *Thaayaar Sannidhi*. Amudan's heart almost stopped. He hid behind the wall and the next time he peeped; he watched the man remove a hammer from his bag and furtively looking around; he struck the lock at the door of the *Thaayaar Sannidhi* and waited. At the next strike, Amudan charged ahead and crouched beneath the raised platform of *Thaayaar Sannidhi*. At the next one, he was right behind the man and before the man could turn around, Amudan landed a fierce blow on the back of his neck with both his hands. The man fell on the floor face down and Amudan sat on the man's back, holding both his hands down.

Seeing no movement or noise from the man, Amudan released one hand and called Manikandan on the phone, asking him to open the temple door.

"Now you can lock the temple" said Amudan, between gasps as he carried the man outside, all his belongings as well, and lay him on the sidewalk outside the temple.

Vasu *Bhattar,* who was still around, peered to take a closer look at the man.

"He is breathing, he is not dead," declared Amudan, watching the horrified expression on Vasu *Bhattar*'s face.

As Amudan called for an ambulance, Manikandan fretfully asked, "*Anna*, shall I call Kumaran *Anna*?"

"We must call the police," added Vasu *Bhattar*.

"Call everyone," said Amudan with a steely glance at Vasu *Bhattar*.

Soon the crowd gathered and Vasu *Bhattar*, without any enquiry or confirmation, spread the word around, "Amudan struck this fellow down. We don't know if he is unconscious or dead."

The crowd stood scattered around, dropping deadly glances at Amudan. The cops and Kumaran arrived first and almost together. They heard Amudan narrate the incident in full. Manikandan and his friend left in the ambulance with the man, while Kumaran left for the police station with Amudan.

The police, on inspection of the shrine of the Goddess, found that the lock looked tampered with but was not broken. Amudan clarified that the lock was struck three times and before the next strike of the hammer, he had attacked the man from behind.

The man had carried just a screwdriver and a hammer in his bag, along with a purse and a phone. There was no other evidence of an attempted burglary other than Amudan's word for it.

Further on enquiry, Vasu Bhattar confirmed that the man had been regularly attending the daily poojas, three times a day for about a week and unreservedly vouched for the stranger to be, "*a devout, humble man.*"

On the other hand, Amudan had been keeping a watchful eye on the man since the last time he had found him near the *Goshala* around the temple closing time. His furtive look and fidgety movements, when spotted, were disconcerting to Amudan.

"Amuda, you are lucky that guy is alive. You should have stopped him or called for help, even if you suspected him of being a burglar. You shouldn't have hit him," remarked the Sub-Inspector of Police. Amudan's remorseless expression was only complicating the situation.

Much to their relief, they soon heard from the hospital that the man had regained consciousness.

The police enquiry was still on and there were only reports from the temple circles that said that Amudan was known for his quick temper and high-handed behaviour.

As Amudan, Kumaran and Ramanujam were still at the police station with a lawyer, much to their bewilderment, the local Minister walked in with his men. His hurried steps and the anxious glance he cast on Amudan only left them more unsettled.

"This boy is known to me," began the Minister as Kumaran hesitantly took a few steps closer to him.

With a gentle pat on Kumaran's shoulder, the Minister turned to the police officer and said, "These two boys guard the temple and the town and it is our duty to give them due protection, isn't it?"

Undertaking personal responsibility for Amudan, the Minister requested the officer to relieve Amudan immediately. Watching Ramanujam stand up with his hands folded, the Minister held his hands saying, "I owe your son much more!"

His encounter with Amudan a few months earlier had been haunting him, reminding him of his family's vow two generations back. The Minister's ancestral house was purchased by his grandfather from a devout Brahmin, a Vedic scholar who had been serving at the temple. While agreeing to sell the property to the Minister's grandfather, the Vedic scholar had said, "*I have served this Perumal till the time my limbs were able to carry me. Now I am leaving this town dependent on my son. I would never like to sell this house because Perumal has come and stood at the door so many times. To me, our Perumal is my first son. Promise me that you will offer him fruits and flowers every time he comes here.*" The Minister's grandfather had readily consented to it with a heartfelt vow to carry on the tradition and pass it on for generations to come.

He lived by his word and the tradition continued until the Minister's father moved out of the town. The custom of visiting the town during festivals also dwindled over the years. Amudan's words came as a loud reminder of his duty and debt and the Minister grew hesitant to proceed with the property sale.

The Minister finally called off the sale once he heard that his son, who was married for over fifteen years, was expecting his first child, at last.

A boon, that all the tonnes of his wealth couldn't buy! With that, the family reclaimed their ties to the ancestral property, the town, the temple and the deities. They finally found out where their treasure trove lay!

A few days later, Kumaran received a call from the Sub-Inspector saying the man spotted at the temple had been involved in burglaries in five other temples in South India over the last six years as confirmed by the fingerprints that matched and that he was immediately arrested.

The incident created quite a stir. For one, Vasu *Bhattar* grew quieter from then on, while Amudan's friends, Manikandan and the other boys, couldn't be quietened from trumpeting all day about Amudan's gallantry.

Blessings come in many forms. Adversity and pain are indeed the most powerful of them. That too when it strikes very close to home, you understand yourself, your shortcomings and the people around you in a way you will never forget.

Vasu *Bhattar*, with his daughter's life taking a complete turn all of a sudden, tragedy and turmoil rocking their boat, now had a lot to reflect upon.

He has served in temples for most of his life, a fact which he often gloated over with unabated pride. For someone who believed that he always held a moral high ground in any given circumstance, and who had looked down upon every other person, with only their faults glaring at him, his pride and self-righteous nature, left him with more adversaries and hardly any friends.

Even as his wife kept prodding him to seek help, he had shunned it, saying, *"I would rather starve my family to death!"*

Vasu *Bhattar* stood outside the shrine of *Thaayaar,* his eyes brimming with tears, his own words ringing in his ears!

Overcome by emotions, he stood before the Goddess, wiping the stream of tears he could hardly control. "*I am not here crying out of devotion or from any exalted spiritual experience. Far from it, I am just an ordinary helpless mortal, a father who cannot bear to see his child suffer.*" He thought and wept like a child.

"*I have never aspired for anything that was beyond my means. I don't remember even praying for the well-being of my family. I have been diligent in the deliverance of my duties every day of my service in the temple. I have never harmed or wronged anyone, to my knowledge. What am I being punished for, Amma?*" he pined with all his heart.

He was jolted by the noise of footsteps approaching. As he hastened to wipe his eyes with the ends of his *angavasthram*, his eyes met those of Amudan, rustling in with a huge Pooja vessel perched on his shoulder.

Vasu *Bhattar* stood blankly staring at Amudan, his thoughts racing. While Amudan noticing the tear-laden eyes of Vasu *Bhattar*, brusquely looked away.

By a surge of strength, a wild gush of courage that rose from nowhere or just the force of divine will," Amudan!" Vasu Bhattar called, his voice shaking with desperation.

Amudan stopped and turned to Vasu *Bhattar*, looking at the latter incredulously, finding his gesture and tone quite unusual.

"You might have heard about it. My son-in-law, Varadan was running a catering business in Madurai. He was doing very well. A few months back in a wedding contract he was catering for, there was a jewellery theft that had occurred and it was found one of his men had stolen it. That boy had dragged my son-in-law into it. Although my son-in-law was innocent and there was no proof of his involvement in the theft, his reputation was lost at once. He has not had any contracts for almost a year. No one would even employ him anymore. Without any hope, he had once even attempted to kill himself, Amuda," he said as he choked with tears. "*Perumal* has protected the family right in time. They are shattered, Amuda. They don't have the will to fight anymore! They are penniless now and unable to sustain themselves in the city. With no place else to go, they have now moved to Kumbakonam and are living in my house…" said Vasu Bhattar and stood looking at Amudan, unable to go on.

"I will come home tonight," replied Amudan, seeing Vasu *Bhattar* weak with emotions and struggling for words.

Nodding gratefully, Vasu *Bhattar,* with his voice trembling said, "I have no one else I can talk to about this. Or ask for help." Amudan's impassive gaze was all the kindness Vasu *Bhattar* needed.

Later that evening, after the *pooja* at the temple, Amudan got a call from a friend abroad.

"My friend's parents are coming down to Kumbakonam on a pilgrimage, starting from Kasi. They want to spend a month in Kumbakonam visiting nearby temples. They are very orthodox people. My friend wanted to know if we can arrange accommodation in Kumbakonam and home-cooked meals for them." Amudan readily offered to help and strolled off to Vasu Bhattar's house.

Vasu Bhattar was still at the temple and his wife and daughter greeted and received Amudan.

With no introduction or any word of courtesy or comfort, Amudan, in his typical plain and placid manner, spoke to the ladies, "We have a family who will be visiting Kumbakonam next week. They will be staying at my brother-in-law's house. They need home-cooked meals for the one month while they will be staying here. Can Varadan *Anna* help?" he asked.

Before Vasu Bhattar's wife and daughter could take in his words, Varadan, who was lying down in a dark corner inside, sprang up to his feet and emerged out, unkempt and haggard. He could only nod his assent, hardly able to utter a word! They all stood dazed and speechless as they watched Amudan take leave and unassumingly walk out of their door, leaving his phone number with Varadan.

With that, Varadan's initiation into home catering services happened almost overnight as the official caterer for the guests of Ranganathan's homestay in the town. This attracted more guests to the homestay and more contacts for Varadan. That humble family slowly regained their morale and their roots.

The Jolt

It was the day of *Ekadesi,* and arrangements were underway for the *Thirumanjanam* of Lord Sarangapani. People of the town slowly gathered and were seated around the *mandapam* where the event was to take place.

Amudan emerged from behind a screen around the *mandapam* and flung a garland right into the flower basket placed on the ground.

"Amudan, why did you throw away this garland?" shot Komala, taking the flower basket in her hand.

“The flowers aren't fresh,” he replied casually.

"What do you mean? Not every flower will be the same. Some fade faster!" she explained.

"I don't know all that. The flowers have got to be fresh. That's all!" he replied.

"And who are you to decide that?" she scowled. "Who are you to decide which garland should reach the Lord's neck and which shouldn't? Can you ever look beyond the form? Every flower was made into this garland so they reach the Lord before they die. You can understand nothing of that and just plainly cast the garland away?" she questioned.

Indeed, he couldn't understand anything of what she was saying. He plainly stood staring at her.

" Arrogance! Who are you, by the way? Who gave you the authority to come in between *Perumal* and his devotees? You treat us all with so much disrespect. Can you even recite a line of a *Pasuram,* one *Sloka*? What if the Lord inside looked at you with the same critical eyes as yours? It will not take a moment for you to be thrown out of the temple in the same way as these flowers, mind you," she thundered.

Watching some of the flowers spill out of her hands, Amudan gestured to her to pick them up. Overcome with rage, she dropped the whole basket down, staring back at Amudan defiantly.

"Amuda, there is a limit, and you have gone way beyond it. Be warned! ,"

As the girl next to her bent down to pick up the basket, Komala said, "You will not touch it. We know how and when to clean it up. No one will tell us how to do it! Don't be scared of him! What will he do now? Will he also throw me out?" She challenged.

"This is our temple, each one of ours. Not his exclusive property for him to run it on his terms." The crowd all stood watching this, some nodding and murmuring their approval, others still in shock.

Watching Kumaran enter at a distance, Amudan slowly moved to leave.

"Amuda! Where are you going?" she asked.

Showing the silver pot in his hand, he said, "I have work!"

"Wait, I am not done! You cannot walk out that way when I am talking to you. Learn some respect!" she said and watched Kumaran walk into the scene and Manikandan whispering into his ears.

"All of us are here to serve at the temple. No one is superior to another, understand? While you have nowhere other than this temple to go to, think about it!" She was hardly in control of herself anymore.

"We are all merely tolerating you, Amudan! Please bear that in mind."

" You have neither an educational qualification nor a job worth the name, I am curious where you got this arrogance from! After all the cleaning you do around the temple, perhaps you have carried much of the dirt over to your head. Do you even treat this place with the kind of respect it deserves? You shout at the devotees, the *Archakas* and the poor volunteers dancing to your tunes. Including this one" she said, pointing to Kumaran.

"Komala, that's enough!" muttered Kumaran, who was still in shock. Amudan gripped his hand tight.

"That's enough, Kumaran! You better realise that. You and my father are the ones who have blindly indulged him this far. He will be nobody without you both. Has he ever stood up for you? Has it ever bothered him what people talk about you in the town? You are still trusting him to be a friend! He is a nobody! No emotions, no virtues, just a plain, empty-headed ruffian roaming here!" She yelled hysterically.

"One more word," shouted *Bhattar*, barging out of the screen. "Komala, one more word you utter, you will be the one to be thrown out of here! Have you lost your mind? "he reproached, "You stay quiet or leave now!" threatened her father, glowering at her while Kumaran stormed out of the place.

Komala broke into tears at that and left with a huff, bundling up the flowers and the basket in her hands.

The incident quite pained them all! Even Amudan.

That afternoon, Amudan was overseeing the construction work at the *Goshala*. While the workers had stepped out for lunch, Amudan was stretched on a huge heap of sand under the shade of a large Bodhi tree. Komala's words and her tear-laden eyes still lingered in his mind.

"*Why wouldn't Perumal kick me out of here when all I do is hurt his devotees?*" Amudan pondered, turning his phone off, lest his mother would start calling him over for lunch. With the gentle breeze caressing him, his eyes slowly drew shut and Amudan dozed off a bit in deep thought.

"*Amuda! Amuda*!" He heard his father's voice.

He woke up with a start.

"Come home. We got a call from Padma. She has been trying to reach you. *Athimber* has been admitted to the hospital. He is in the critical care unit. They say it might be a heart attack." His father's voice was shaking as he said those words.

Amudan sprang up to his feet at that. He ran like a madman to their house, while turning his phone on. He trembled to hear Padma's voice muffled with shock and fear. She was barely audible. Amudan, along with the rest of the family, rushed to Chennai in a friend's cab.

With severe blocks in the arteries, Ranganathan was headed for an attack which was thwarted right in time. After a few days of treatment and observation in the critical care unit, Ranganathan was shifted to the normal ward. While Ranganathan's brother shuttled back and forth to the hospital during the day, Amudan stayed at the hospital at night.

Ranganathan was still coming to terms with the altered circumstances, all too suddenly. Even as he was too dazed to hold any cogent line of thought, a strange sense of fear seemed to have crawled under his skin and spread all over. There was no physical pain. He was out of danger, he could see from Padma's smile. Only one thing, he couldn't now look her in the eye!

If there was some relief, it was watching Amudan walk in every evening with Padma.

Amudan's laid-back demeanour, his simple attire, an old T-shirt and white dhoti folded up to his knees, his candidness and child-like agility, everything about him, felt balmy! He could rest whenever he chose to anyway, but having Amudan beside him was itself a restful state. Ranganathan could feel more at ease with himself.

It was a warmth that he had never felt with any friend or even with his brother. There was no compulsion to talk, but Ranganathan had so much to tell him, every night. He spoke about Padma and Sarangan, his parents and brother, his childhood and his work.

Amudan paid an attentive audience to him, neither too eager nor disinterested and never judgemental. Amudan's expression hardly changed. He quietly heard Ranganathan out until they retired to bed each night.

Watching Amudan meekly cuddle and squirm under the blanket on the side couch, Ranganathan could see how unaccustomed to comfort Amudan was! He would switch off the air-conditioner now and then and watch on!

For Amudan, his comfort lay elsewhere. It was the first time in many years he was away from the temple for almost a week. He spoke to Kumaran almost every hour of the day, to Narayana *Bhattar* several times a day, and to Manikandan and the boys at the temple to check on them or just to hear the temple bells.

Needless to say, it was immense strength for Padma to have her family around in these difficult times. Watching Amudan scuttle around the house, cleaning or fixing one thing or the other, and playing with Sarangan was enough to lift her spirits. He dropped and picked up Sarangan from school every day on a bike or by walk, as he chose.

"Amuda, you have no idea how it feels to have you here," said Padma. "Sarangan thinks you will stay with us forever," she went on with a chuckle.

"*Athimber* is so happy, I know. Amuda, will you stay with us? At least for some more time, till *Athimber* fully recovers?"

Amudan merely nodded. Did she even know what she was asking for? As for Amudan, there was nothing more he could ask for than to see his sister smile in these times, and he couldn't dare to risk that at any cost. At the same time, he could neither rein in his mind that darted away to the deity of his heart, every minute he had to himself, while he ate or rested.

"Have Thaayaar and Perumal forgotten me? Or are they punishing me?" he often wondered and lay awake at night. Komala's words were indeed still playing in his mind.

No one knew the pain he quietly bore. His family could only see that he was there for them, whirling about in action, doing all that he could, wherever he was needed.

All their hearts were full, indeed, and Ramanujam's hopes for his son were all stoked up again! All said, how much could have Amudan hidden from his mother?

Perundevi only watched his plate. She could see how he struggled through one course of a meal each time. She never dared to look into his eyes. She made sure he was kept busy all day.

One evening, Amudan, who had gone to fetch Sarangan from school, walked in calling for Perundevi, "*Amma,* do you want to see *Perumal* on the *Garudan*?" When she turned to look at him, she saw Sarangan perched on Amudan's shoulders and Amudan, holding the little one's feet in his palms, like the *Garuda Azhwar,* and stood smiling at her. She lost all her grit to that smile!

Ranganathan had made a good recovery and with every day of progress, he gathered more energy to dispense with and was only tired of the hospital bed.

It was the evening before discharge, Amudan walked in carrying dinner for Ranganathan while the latter was on a business call.

The call went on for the next thirty minutes and never seemed to end, even when Ranganathan's voice was turning frail and beginning to shake.

Amudan couldn't wait any longer. He grabbed the phone from Ranganathan switched it off and put it aside, paying no heed to Ranganathan's meek requests for his phone.

"*Porum*!" muttered Amudan. Ranganathan sat staring at Amudan, still shocked but helpless. He had bills to pay, many families to feed, his suppliers to answer, and Padma and Sarangan to protect. While there was a man who stood before him, assumed full authority over him, to grab his phone, his time and opportunity, all in one go, staring back at him, right into his eyes with indignation.

Although Amudan was only ten years younger than him, he looked much younger and more spirited to him than his ten-years younger self. He felt at that moment that he had lost much more than he had gained in those years. Amudan's stern look, a tinge of retribution in it, seemed to punish him for that. That gnawing sense of fear that he had pushed under the rug for so long was now glaring at him hard! He felt his time was dearer now. The fear of it being grabbed from him was more real. He hung his head down.

"*Athimber*, are you hungry?" He heard Amudan's soft voice and turned to look at him.

"I have never told Padma how well she cooks," said Ranganathan, looking up at Amudan from his plate, choking on his words.

"I have not told her many things, Amuda. She does not know how much I earn or how much savings we have."

He looked at Amudan longer this time, perhaps hoping Amudan would have something to say. He could only see the same pristine expression he would find on Padma's face.

"She has done a lot for me, Amuda. I could not have come this far without her. My life was only about my business but for her..," his eyes brimmed with tears as Amudan stepped closer to hold the plate for him. "Her world revolves around Sarangan and me. I have not been very kind." He trailed off again.

"Why do you think about all this now, *Athimber*?" asked Amudan, taking the plate from his hands.

"What if I had no more time, Amuda? I have worked well, earned well, and saved enough for my family. They can sustain well even without me! I want more time with them now. I want to see Sarangan getting married. He is only six years old! Padma wanted to do his *Upanayanam* next year. There is a lot of money left, I might not have time left, I am afraid!" He shook with tears. Amudan held his shoulders tight, not knowing what to say.

Gathering himself, "Can you pray for me?" He asked

"You are all right, Athimber. Once you go home and eat well, you will get stronger. Don't worry! *Perumal* will take care of everything. "

Both Amudan and Ranganathan could hardly sleep that night.

The next morning, Padma and Ramanujam arrived at the hospital to relieve Amudan. As Amudan took leave, Ranganathan asked, "When are you leaving for Kumbakonam, Amuda?"

Before Amudan could respond, Padma said, "What is the hurry now? He will go after you settle down well at home." "Correct. Let him stay for a few more days," seconded Ramanujam.

"I will settle down just fine, Padma. Will take my own time but we have to set this bird free soon! Right away! I don't like to take any more of his time," said Ranganathan with a wink at Amudan. Amudan's eyes blooming into a smile, he left, closing the door behind him.

Sunrise

It was much easier than expected to convince Padma about Amudan leaving.

She could hardly contain her joy as she said to Amudan, "*Athimber* wants to come to Kumbakonam for the ten-day festival next month, *Da*. He wants to spend a relaxed time with all of us there. Pray it happens, Amuda."

Perundevi was the hardest for Amudan to deal with. Ever since she heard about Komala's showdown at the temple, she was boiling with rage, though she kept it to herself. She knew it was no use speaking to Amudan about it. Her anguish and pain only seemed to grow with time and even their move to Chennai and the circumstances that ensued couldn't much insulate her mind from the incident. If at all, it only flamed her animosity towards Ranganayaki and Komala all the more.

As Amudan bid her adieu, he stood, shocked, as she said, "Amuda, promise me you will not step into Ranganayaki's house again."

"How can I promise all that, *Amma*? Why? What has happened now?" He asked, perplexed.

"I know what happened. No one can shout at you like that, Amuda. Anyway, you will not understand all this. Just remember not to go and eat at their house, even if Ranganayaki asks you to. I want you to cook your meals at home till I come home. Will you do that?" She asked and heaved a sigh of relief as he nodded.

Ramanujam and Perundevi were to leave back home in a week's time.

Darkness and lull were slowly making their way to the first streaks of daybreak. The doors of every house in the town slowly shrieked open, one after another. Cows were mooing aloud, beckoning their calves to feed on their milk, the jingle of the bells around their necks, more frenzied with joy! The healing scent of the dew-wet sand, the sound of the birds chirping with hope, in delight of another day before them. The rays of relief and sereneness spread all around, as the sun rose again in their town!

Komala was sweeping the entrance of their house, softly reciting the *Thirupalli ezhuchi.* She could see from the corner of her eye- a flash of something white. Instantly she turned to the road and watched Amudan approaching, his *Thiruman Sricharanam* shimmering bright and the pristine white *angavastram* draped around waving to his sprightly gait. With the *dhoti* folded up to his knees, his firm and long strides were more pronounced. Like a crown prince taking a triumphant march back to his cherished kingdom!

Komala stood up, stopping midway through her *Kolam,* and waited for Amudan to enter their house. He walked up to the entrance and halted with a sudden change of mind and, stepping to the side, perched himself on the *Thinnai*. His mother's words brushed by his mind.

As always, he paid no attention to her presence. Komala finishing the *kolam,* rushed into the house and whispered to her father, "Amudan has come!"

Bhattar leapt to his feet and hurried out calling, "Amuda!" Amudan, hearing *Bhattar*'s voice, jumped out of the *Thinnai* and sprinted into their house.

"Come, Amuda! When did you come?" enquired *Bhattar* when Amudan coyly smiling, replied, "Just a while back."

While *Bhattar* and Ranganayaki were enquiring at length about Ranganathan's health, Komala sat stringing a garland.

When it was time to leave for the temple, Amudan gathered the flower garlands in the large basket and patiently stood waiting as Komala rushed to finish the last one.

As she handed him the Lotus garland, their eyes met for a fraction of a second. It was a moment enough to tell that he carried *no anger, hate or grudge*.

She recalled the words of her father the evening after the incident.

*"It is not easy to understand Amudan. Every day we recite the pasuram, "Aaravamude Adiyen..." where Azhwar says, "Neeraay alaindhu karaiya urukkuginra nedumale". You may know the bare meaning of the words. But have we really understood the import of even the word, "Adiyen.." beyond the common parlance? Can we ever endeavour to imagine the depth of devotion to the Lord, as Azhwar says, "I have completely melted and dissolved in your insatiable sweetness and love." How can we even understand what it is to melt and dissolve, from a place of ego, where we stand? Amudan threw away the garland that "**I** "made!*

Amudan may not even know a line of the pasuram, much less its meaning but his devotion to the Lord has moulded him from within. Till there is nothing left to melt. She recalled how her father choked on his words as he went on." *At some point, the child lost all sensations of pain. I have seen him through it at every stage. I am not sure your education can ever mould a person that way! He may look like a ruffian to all of us. The tenderness of his heart is way too much for you to imagine. There is no limit to how far he can stretch himself in service to the temple, to this town, and each of us here. Never fool yourself into thinking that Kumaran and I are the ones protecting him. I trust your devotion to the Lord will, with time, enlighten you more! But remember one thing, for all that you have spoken about him, he will hold no anger, hate or grudge! That is Amudan!*"

Truer words have never been spoken!

People around could only see Amudan's grim countenance, grave temper, and harsh words. Like a slender wick holding the burning fire, not many could look through his fiery façade enough to notice the tenderness beneath. He was a child put through harsh parenting, who had dealt with physical and emotional assaults from a tender age. All that while he was fighting to be himself and to follow his heart, no matter what. Those traumatic years sure left him with many bruises, including a rough and tough exterior.

There were many bottled-up emotions within him waiting to explode, anytime. For all the aggression and ferocity he exhibited, now and then, he could have well turned into an unscrupulous, destructive personality, a menace to the society but for the ONE he had held dear in his heart! The one who steered the rest of his life. Lord Aravamudan, his muse, his master, and his only mission!

Amudan's love for the Lord only grew with age until it could no longer be contained within his heart. He sculpted the idol of the Lord all night and day, served at the temple, cleaned its premises, he did all he could to find an expression of his love which only kept growing beyond, unsatiated. It was an unending stream that overflowed into everything he did, to everyone he came across; whether he tended the cows or the dogs or ploughed the fields, it was this unbounded love that flowed through him, touching every life around him.

Drowned in this wild gush of love, Amudan hardly existed those moments and was oblivious to any pain or pleasure inflicted on him and as much blind to the people who may have caused it. For he had lost all of himself to the Divine form!

Life still happened for Amudan, undiminished. Steadfast in his role as a son, a brother, a friend to anyone in need, though all he really was - a mere captive, a pliable instrument in the hands of his Master! His emotions of anger, fear and joy, his sensations of pain and pleasure, were held hostage too! Even the wild rage that washed over him, they all merely passed through him like they were meant to. Like seasons that come and go, at the right time and in the right measures!

He was never bound by them. He remained untarnished, holding *no anger, hate or grudge!*

Amudan, though, never sat back to reflect on his own life. Where he had started, where he was headed, or how far he had come. There was just one thing he knew, there was no place else that he would rather be! *It felt like home*, he thought, taking a stroll around the temple.

Amudan was at the *Goshala,* tending to the cows, one after the other, as they mooed aloud, nodding their heads, longing for his touch and attention. He could spend hours that way in their quiet company, licked and loved to their hearts' content.

"Amuda, when did you come?" asked Malli as she stood behind watching the dear sight of Amudan fondly resting his forehead on that of a cow, gently scratching its neck and staring right into its eye.

Turning to Malli, he replied, "This morning!" His eyes cringed with concern, seeing her look so haggard and weak. She was six months pregnant.

"Everything ok? Murthy is in town?" he inquired.

Overcome by fear, she said, "I don't know where he is. I have not seen him since last evening when he came home drunk again. He beat me up badly," she said and began to weep.

"Then he left and has not come home till now. I am worried. I came to see the *Paalkaara Anna* to check if he saw my husband somewhere."

"Stop worrying and go home!" snapped Amudan. "He will come home to hit you again. Where will he go? Can you not live in peace even until then?" he sputtered as he dialled Murthy's number. The call didn't go through.

"You give me a call once he gets home. I will break his legs this time. He will not touch you again!" he hissed as he stormed out.

Amudan had asked a few volunteers to look for Murthy while Malli returned to her flower stall. Amudan had also arranged for someone to mind the flower shop so she could take some time off and rest.

About noon, when the *Uchikaala* Pooja was on, one of the volunteers rushed to him in panic.

"*Anna*, they found Murthy *Annan*'s body in a well near their house. The police are there. He was drunk and had fallen into the well they are saying." Amudan and Kumaran sped to the spot the next moment.

Not a drop of tears in her eyes. Was she in a state of shock? Was she too drained of tears? Nobody could say, as the rest of the women around were howling and crying, grieving over the dead man, his pregnant wife, and his unborn child. She silently watched them all. The last rites were done and mourners all wound up tired. She was still sitting in the same place.

She watched from afar Amudan and Kumaran, getting ready to leave. Amudan was there all day, she knew, but he never came in to see her. He couldn't gather enough courage for that. Amudan, noticing Malli looking towards him, walked over to her.

"He cannot touch me again," she said, staring hard at Amudan.

"He beat me up! He kicked me so many times that night! "*Who will come to save you?* " he asked. He shouted, "*Go, call Amudan, now*!" Even before you could come, he was gone! He will not touch me again! He can never touch my child! He is gone!" she screamed hysterically and began to wheeze wildly.

The women around rushed to her side to pacify her. Amudan was standing shell-shocked, watching her battle for her breath.

When Malli regained consciousness, she found herself in a hospital. "How is the child?" she asked the nurse and was relieved to know that all was well.

She had no family in this town. Her parents were dead long ago. Her husband's relatives must have all left for their towns after the funeral. She realised that she and her unborn child were all alone from now on. A strange fear gripped her mind.

Just then, she recalled Amudan's eyes, watching her on as she was gasping for breath. He was the one she had fought the most! She couldn't believe that he was the only one now who even cared that she was alive. Why? For what purpose? She couldn't even string a garland for the condition she was in. He ran the flower shop for her, bought and sold the flowers and gave her the daily earnings. He protected her like it was his duty, like a soldier on guard. But why?

Who was she to him? What use, what purpose did he find in her when she could find nothing herself?

Closing her eyes, she ran her hand over her abdomen, trying to feel and reach out to the one resting in her womb. *Indeed, I have a purpose too,* she thought as tears welled in her eyes. *It was to deliver the child!*

With strict instructions for bed rest and nourishment, she was discharged in a couple of days. Amudan never visited her, but all her needs were taken care of. She had a lot of visitors every day.

Amudan made sure the temple *prasadam*, three times a day, reached Malli on time. He made it the town's responsibility to nourish Malli. He would never shrug to ask Ranganayaki or Desikan's mother, "Can you make something healthy for Malli?" Perundevi after her return to town, made sure to reserve an extra portion for Malli as every time Amudan sat down to eat, he would stop her as she served him and ask, "Amma, can you save some for Malli?"

He had arranged for an old woman to stay with her at night and some others to accompany her to the doctor. Komala was overjoyed watching her mother take a special interest in Malli. She frequented Malli's house carrying one thing or the other her mother would send. Despite Malli's health issues, these were the best memories of her life.

Overwhelmed with gratitude, she once told Komala, "I hope this child makes you all proud. Even before being born, the child owes so much to you all!" Komala was moved to tears by the words. She could hardly imagine the state of the woman's mind!

Komala visited her more often. They spoke a lot about many things and found so much to share, learn and laugh about. When she spoke of Amudan though, Malli choked with emotions every time.

She once said to Komala, "He might have been my brother or my mother in a previous birth, as they say! In this birth, I know for sure, he is my God!" and wept her heart out. "Who else would care so much without a reason, to protect a poor orphan like me?"

With all her strength and resolve, Malli sat glowing like a saint in penance each day.

A wild turn

"This whole town is spinning around one pregnant woman! Have you seen anything like this? Especially Amudan *Anna*. He has only not carried *Thaayaar* and *Perumal* to Malli's house," lamented Sowmya.

"Amudan is very soft-hearted. He will help anyone who is in need," replied Govindan.

"Oh, is it? I have never seen his soft side in a long time. Perhaps I need to get pregnant for that. He is only tougher with me. The last time when we had friends from my hometown visiting the temple, he embarrassed me by saying, "*Follow the queue!*" They all asked if I were not allowed to entertain even a few friends now and then."

"If only you were serving at the temple in my hometown, we would be leading an altogether different life!" She said dreamily as she coiled on Govindan's lap. He gently caressed her hair with all the warmth he could give her.

"What do we lack here, Sowmya? We now have all the comforts you asked for, and so many people around to help us. More than anything, we live in the shadow of *Perumal* and *Thaayaar.* What more do you want? "

"Enough! Don't utter a word more!" she scowled as she rose to sit. "Did you have the money to buy even one of that? For everything, we have to look up to Amudan and Kumaran!

They also live in the shadow of *Perumal* and *Thaayaar. Where* do they get their money from? You are neither smart nor can you be taught to be. It is my life that is ruined! If you wanted only *Perumal* and *Thaayaar*, why did you even get married? If you are not interested in material things, then why marry? It is all my bad luck. I can only blame my father. My destiny!" she said as she sniffled.

They heard the entrance door screech open. Watching Amudan walk into the house, Sowmya sprung up to her feet and stormed into the kitchen, mumbling.

Govindan, unable to look Amudan in the eye, hung his head down while the latter quietly plonked by his side.

The rattle of vessels in the kitchen grew louder, and she let out a cry, "Are you coming to eat? I have cooked only for the two of us," she added.

"Amuda! Can you come later?" whispered Govindan hesitantly, his face red with shame.

Amudan nodded and made his way out.

Govindan was heartbroken after the incident. He kept to his temple duties, and engaged in longer *Archana* for *Thaayaar,* but avoided eye contact with anyone, especially Amudan. He ate the *prasadam* at the temple and went home only late at night. His pain-stricken eyes were an unbearable sight to Amudan.

When Amudan could no longer take it, he confronted Govindan. "What is wrong? Is anything bothering you? I heard you don't eat at home. Sowmya was worried."

Staring at Amudan long and hard, "Why should you be worried? Who are you? It is my life. I will handle it. You have done enough for me and now I am bearing the brunt of it," said Govindan, folding his hands together.

"What are you saying?" asked Amudan with deep concern.

"Did I ask you to get me married? Do you know what chaos you have landed me in? Just leave, Amuda," he said, shutting his eyes tight.

"What happened?" prodded Amudan. "Whatever it is, tell me!"

"There is nothing left to happen. We should not have been married at all! I cannot satisfy her in any way. I have ruined her life, and that is eating me up more than anything. You cannot understand any of this, Amuda! You will neither let us be. I.... I only wish I could die soon! So I could set her free." He sputtered and wept like a child burying his head between his folded legs.

Amudan shuddered as he stood watching him.

Gathering himself, Govindan turned to Amudan and with a firm look, he said, "I can take care of myself. You please leave me alone! I don't need your sympathies or your help. Nobody is an orphan here, remember? I may not be rich, but will never be an orphan. They are there for me," he muttered, pointing to the shrine of Goddess.

"You better watch your ways, though, Amuda! Money and power have only caused more destruction than good. Watch it!" Govindan warned and looked away.

Amudan seated himself beside Govindan, too shocked and numb, while the latter sprang up to his feet and stormed away.

Sowmya was the one though who suffered the most. Govindan never touched even a drop of milk she offered, never spared her even a glance. Unfazed by her tears, fervent pleas or loud cries, he walked in and out of the house, each day like an ascetic, unaffected by his surroundings. While his sombre and impermeable countenance left her in jitters, in a constant state of shock and panic.

Memories of his affectionate gestures and his ever-indulgent ways kept swinging back to her mind. "*Do I not exist for him anymore?*" she trembled as she thought. She couldn't dare enough to believe that all of his benevolence and untainted love for her had dried up overnight! She couldn't bring herself to open up to anyone about this. Even Ranganayaki's direct and discreet enquiries couldn't pierce through the solemn silence she held, leaving Ranganayaki unusually more worried than curious.

Unkempt and draped in a dull, crumpled saree, she was resigned to a corner of the house, dewy-eyed all day. She had not seen his warm, benign smile for days now! She cried herself to sleep each night, at the sight of Govindan cuddled in a far corner, near their Pooja.

Unrest and anguish, simmering in each of their hearts, an ominous vacuum was all that was looming large.

Early one morning ...

"Bolt the doors!" commanded Amudan. Volunteers, grim with shock, rushed hither and tither to ensure that all the entry and exit points at the temple were shut.

The *Archakas*, all ashen-faced, were huddling up in hushed conversations, some terrified, some others in tears. With hazy, half-information trickling out, there was commotion and panic among the devotees inside the temple.

It was a search operation at the temple that was in progress.

The diamond nose ring of Goddess Komalavalli was noticed to be missing soon after the *Suprabhatha pooja*.

They searched every nook and corner, every shred of flower or dust that was removed from the shrine since the previous night, and every *Archaka* and volunteer thoroughly frisked and their homes searched.

It was almost a day and after an unsuccessful search, there was still tension and panic on all their faces. The nose ring must have gotten lost and not stolen, was the conclusion they all resigned to. No thief would have stolen just the nose ring was their premise.

Govindan was engrossed in the reading of Ramayana, seated in his usual place right outside the shrine of *Thaayaar*. Govindan's unruffled calmness even in these circumstances and a noticeable indifference to the whole thing was quite disturbing for Amudan. Especially given that he was the most interrogated of all, being responsible for the shrine of *Thaayaar*.

Kumaran, on the other hand, could never get around to understanding the sudden strain in their relationship. He only grew more tired of hearing Amudan reply, "Nothing!" every time he was asked if anything was wrong between them.

Amudan was burning with anxiety all day. He could neither rest nor move on. With Govindan's continued cold disposition towards him, Amudan could hardly manage to have any open-hearted discussion with him. Feeling more suffocated with every passing day, he walked into Govinda's house early that morning.

Govindan was in the middle of his daily *Aradanai* to the idols of *Salagramam*, chanting the *Purushasuktham* in his clear unhurried tone. Amudan decided to wait.

Govindan finally recited the *pasuram* "*Aaravamude adiyen,*" his voice quivering with emotion and mounted the sandalwood case carrying the *Salagramam* idols back to its place. Amudan, who until then was sitting on a railing and watching on, walked in closer. He prostrated before the idols of *Salagramam* and waited to be served the *theertham* when something glittering from the sandalwood case caught his eye!

Amudan's eyes widened with shock at what he saw. He could hardly breathe, talk or even move a limb. His fiery, red eyes were fixed on the diamond nose ring glittering from the sandalwood box.

Lost and Found

There was anger, disappointment, pain and tears in Amudan's eyes as he stood like a sculpture made of rock. Govindan, parched and shivering, slowly shook his head, watching Amudan.

"I didn't take it, Amuda! I would never take it," he whispered, his eyes raining down tears.

"That night after the *Sayana Aarthi* the nose ring fell on my lap. I tried to put it back. It kept falling on my lap, every time. The nose ring that *Thaayaar* has worn for decades, how will it loosen in a day? I thought she meant to give it to me. A mother's legacy for me. Like she meant to come to my defence, to say I am no orphan! I was reminded at that moment of Sowmya's daily words of insult asking me, "*How come there is not even a grain of gold or diamond that your mother left behind*?"

He hugged Amudan tight and wept aloud.

"Amuda, will you trust me? I never intended to hold this as just a piece of jewellery. I meant to worship this as a family legacy on par with the *Salagrama* idols in the case. Punish me, however you want, but don't take it away from me, please," he pleaded.

"They searched the whole house that day and left. It was safe in the *Salagramam* case with its lid left ajar all through. I left it to HER will that day, whether she wanted me to hold it or would have it taken away," said Govindan, heaving a deep sigh.

“I cannot understand devotion, Govinda," replied Amudan. "I am too dumb for that! All I know is that this nose ring belongs to *Thaayaar,* and the temple is the only place where it should be. It is our duty now to put it back where it belongs." Thus saying, Amudan stretched his hand out.

"Give it to me!" He ordered.

"I will bring it back myself. I didn't do anything wrong. I can explain, “stuttered Govindan.

"No, you will give it to me and do as I say," threatened Amudan.

"Govinda, there is only one truth. That you did not take it. We will both stand by it and watch whatever ensues as HER will. Is that clear?"

"Give it to me, now!" He compelled with a threatening grimace like he was possessed. Govindan meekly complied.

The moment Govindan placed the nose ring on Amudan's palms, the latter closed his palm over it and said, "Whatever has happened so far will be a secret that we will carry to our ashes. Not another soul will know about it! That's a promise!" he said and stormed out of the house, leaving Govindan in a panic.

Amudan didn't go to Bhattar's house as he usually did, but quietly sat outside the temple, waiting for the town to rise for the day. The doors of houses one after the other shrieked open as women stepped out to draw the *Kolam* at the entrances. Komala and a friend waltzed over to the temple, chatting in whispers, and took turns sweeping and mopping the entrance clean. It was still dark around and well ahead of sunrise. As Komala set out to draw the Kolam, she noticed a pair of legs from the corner of her eyes. She turned to take a closer look and stood up with a start, seeing Amudan there.

It was the second time he had looked into her eyes.

Soon people gathered for the *Suprabhatham* and Komala walked along with *Bhattar* carrying the basket of flowers wondering why Amudan didn't come to fetch the flowers basket today.

As the door opened and *Bhattar* was about to walk into the shrine, Amudan walked closer to him and unfurled his palm before him. He watched *Bhattar*'s eyes bloom with wonder.

"Where did you find it?" he asked, taking the nose ring in his hand. There was a buzz of voices around as people circled them, Vasu *Bhattar* taking a few steps closer.

Amudan didn't answer.

"*Anna*, where was it?" prodded Vasu Bhattar.

"It is here now. It got lost and was found now!" said Amudan to Vasu *Bhattar*.

"We have to know where you found it. This is a question of security. Don't stare back at me! We have to know the full story," said Vasu Bhattar.

The voices around getting louder, Narayana *Bhattar* shook his head as if to warn Amudan and ordered, "Amuda, speak up! Tell me where you found it."

Amudan didn't know what to say. There was only one thing at stake for him. He didn't want to risk saying anything that would even remotely lead them to

Govindan. He couldn't lie as well. He couldn't think. He kept quiet.

"Amuda, you should answer me," threatened Narayan *Bhattar*. Amudan stood with his head hung down.

"If you do not answer, we will have to hand you over to the police," said a person from the crowd.

"He has found the nose ring. What would you want to hand him over for?" demanded another voice.

"You will have to tell us where you found it, Amuda. It will land us all in trouble otherwise," reasoned a trustee. "We have to clear the air on this. If not, we will end up doubting each other."

"*Anna*, it's better to hand this case over to the Police. One police dog can sniff out the truth in no time," suggested Vasu *Bhattar*.

"You try and let a dog inside sniffing around!" threatened Amudan. "What do you want? Do you want to throw me in jail? Go ahead!" yelled Amudan. "Come, let's go!"

"You get out of the temple, now!" thundered Narayana *Bhattar* pointing to Amudan.

"You will not enter the temple again until you speak the truth," he yelled. Amudan looked at him incredulously, least expecting those words from him.

"We will discuss this later, *Anna*," pacified Vasu *Bhattar* and prompted, "It's getting late for *Suprabhatham*."

"Either Amudan has to go out now or I will never enter the temple again!" declared Narayana *Bhattar*, his voice powered with emotions.

Amudan turned around and sprinted out of the temple.

Kumaran, having heard about the happening, came rushing to the temple. He caught Amudan midway as the latter slowed down, catching his breath.

"*Enna da*? Fool! "yelled Kumaran. "Where did you find the nose ring? Why didn't you tell them?"

Amudan pretending to feel dizzy, hopped onto Kumaran's bike saying, "Don't ask me anything, please take me home."

Not having the courage to deal with his father, he begged Kumaran to drive him to the fields.

They sat beneath a tree overlooking the rice fields. The rustle of the soothing breeze, the vast green fields as far as his eyes could reach and Kumaran beside deep in thought, Amudan stretched himself out on the ground and lay quietly just following his breath. Silenced, hustled and ousted, his whole life seemed to have come to a sudden halt in a moment.

Their phones were beeping continuously. Neither of them cared to answer. Amudan mindlessly watched different names flashing on his phone.

Bhooma calling. Padma calling. Athimber calling.

He had nothing to say to anyone. He shut his eyes and lay still.

"Amuda, what is your plan?" asked Kumaran. Amudan merely shook his head.

"NO ONE can ask you to leave the temple, Amuda! Whomever it may be! Come with me now. Don't take this lying low. You have not done anything wrong!"

"Kumara, I cannot come. You leave," snapped Amudan in a soft tone. They stared into each other's eyes long and hard.

"Amuda, don't you trust me? Will you not even tell me where you found it?" He implored.

Amudan quietly looked away. They together have fought many battles. They have trusted each other with their lives and more, no doubt. But is it even trust if it cannot stand its test through words unspoken and actions defying?

Kumaran couldn't rest, stay still for a moment more.

He could bear anything but the weight of the words he had heard, "*Amudan was asked to leave the temple*!" He rose with a jolt and sped to the temple on his bike.

"Who has the right to ask him not to enter the temple?" thundered Kumaran as he watched Narayana *Bhattar* and a few of the trustees and devotees in a huddled discussion.

"Tell me, what are you punishing him for?" he addressed the group.

"Do you think he took the nose ring? I am asking each of you! I dare each one of you here to say it to my face, now, if you think he had stolen it! "

"He cannot hide the truth from us, Kumara. That is wrong!" chipped in Vasu *Bhattar*.

"So! Why don't you find the truth yourself? What stops you? Will you conveniently oust him for that? He found the nose ring, anyway. Or are you punishing him for that?"

"How can you punish him when you know for sure he hasn't stolen the nose ring? Is that justice?" He questioned, walking up to Narayana *Bhattar*.

"How could you ask him to leave? No one but Amudan would have taken it lying low. You know that! He will do anything if you ask him to, *Mama*. So, would you ask him to die?" He choked out.

"I am sorry. I don't have the age or wisdom to advise you, but I know that what you have done is wrong! I will not keep quiet. I will find the truth!"

"I will not rest until I find out the person hiding behind Amudan. I will come back to see all your faces that day!" he vowed with a threatening glance at each one there.

"I swear on, "my" Amudan, I will not step inside this temple until then!" saying, he stormed out.

Chaos

"Fool! Emotional fool!" commented Vasu *Bhattar*. "How will he find out the culprit if he swears not to step into the temple?" while chewing a betel leaf in the company of a friend.

"This is very intriguing, Vasu. Amudan is someone who was close to killing a guy who tried to break open the *Thaayaar Sannidhi* lock. He is a fanatic when it comes to the temple matters. Do you think he will even try to cover up someone who had held the nose ring of *Thaayaar*? He will murder the fellow and go to jail. Who will be the one person Amudan will do this for?" he quizzed.

"Unfortunately, that's the tough part to conclude on. As Amudan would do this for any of us! Without an exception!" said Vasu *Bhattar* with a deep sigh.

He was the one who had always opposed Amudan, most vociferously. He was the one who had wanted Amudan ousted. But today, watching Amudan turn around and quietly walk out of the temple, he shivered with shock and pain. Like it was a lash of whip that fell on him! As much as he didn't approve of Amudan's stand on this, his heart bled more, watching Amudan take the blow.

Amudan didn't walk alone, he thought. He carried with him all their conceit, their false sense of worth, leaving them all too fragile to bear the weight of their conscience.

"Enough! It's good for him! This is the only way we can get him out of the temple affairs. He has wasted enough time. He has to move on in life. Kumara, listen to me. Pack him off to Delhi right away. He will not spend a moment more in that town. No one deserves him there," charged Desikan.

"Why should he go to Delhi? Why should he run away? They send him out of the temple and do you want me to pack him out of the town as well? Amudan will be here and here only unless he wishes otherwise!" replied Kumaran.

"Kumaran, please understand. So long as he is there, all these people will use him. Parasites! No one is ready to stick their necks out for him. After they have all sucked his time and energy out, all these years. Did you see the messages in the group? I will make sure he doesn't hold a Power of Attorney for anyone. A thankless job, anyway! Let them manage their parents, properties and fields by themselves. I will have the trust wound up as well and get his name out of it for good," he went on.

"He owes no one anything, I agree. You do whatever has to be done with the trust and the money. I have no problem with it. I got out of the group, anyway. Couldn't stand their comments and enquiries! " muttered Kumaran.

"That's very convenient! We need to know what each one has to say, especially the cruel minds. I will stay in the group to see the real faces of each one and tear them apart! Plus, I owe Amudan more than anyone here. This whole group happened around my wedding. I will make sure to have it all cleaned up now."

"How is Amudan?" finally inquired Desikan. There was a long phase of silence. It was two days since the incident.

"It is his world, Desika. The temple! It's his home, his life! I cannot imagine his state of mind. He is holding up well, I think. He walks up and down the town, the four streets around the temple all day. He wears himself out working in the fields the rest of the time. "

He trailed off, recalling Amudan's downcast eyes. They had not looked each other in the eye these past few days.

"I only hope he finds the time to introspect," butted in Desikan. "I hope he finally got to see the real face of some of the people he deeply cared for, the *Bhattar* in particular."

"No way! Has it ever mattered to him? Real faces or fake? He only knows that there is no other way he can be! That is our Amudan, isn't it? You can neither fight with anyone the way he does nor help the very same people, the way he does. Everyone knows that! People seldom even thank him these days! He does it as his duty. They say one's good deeds don't fail him. Even the Gods owe him more now, perhaps!" said Kumaran, barely able to go on.

"Definitely! *Komalavalli Thaayaar* more than anyone!" muttered Desikan, turning pensive.

It is in these times of overwhelming grief that one's faith muddled deep under, emerges out, most subconsciously!

Desikan, not a regular to the temple, who had all these years stepped into the temple only looking for his friend, had now made a secret vow to the Goddess that he would take up his family's annual *Mandagapadi* if Amudan was granted entry into the temple again.

For someone who had always thought that respect for life and humanity was the highest form of worship of the creator and who had desisted the custom of visiting the temple for he believed it was a place that harboured more hatred than love, that bred more divide and discrimination than harmony.

The only one he trusted to be above and beyond was Amudan and for the very reason, Amudan was the only one he cared to protect as well.

As much as he was protective of Amudan and wary of his dauntless, seemingly quixotic ways, he was still in awe of Amudan's nature to plunge himself into selfless service to God and humans, even snakes, dogs or cats alike. Amudan couldn't be bound by any of the societal norms or measures. Never too vocal about his views, he made his life a statement, though! That true liberation came not out of being loved and accepted for who you are but being yourself, irrespective!

That kindness and love are not mere manners of expression but the most potent energy that can be silently passed on to another. He saw how Amudan could do that with ease, most dispassionately like it was his duty, his habit!

His love and admiration for Amudan only grew with years beyond their differences and despite the things he could never understand or come to terms with. So much that he only wished he could love all the things that were dear to Amudan.

What's more with Bhooma entering his life! Her playfulness and affectionate gestures kindled and brought out all the tenderness left in him.

He could now see more of the tender side of things, of people, of God and the temple as well! Dusting off his biases and strong opinions, he could look through a clear lens of fairness and justice. He could see not just the fallacies of mankind but the restraint and judiciousness of the creator, playing a benevolent parent and an impartial judge in balancing good and evil. In giving each one equal freedom and chances and making them accountable for their actions.

He could understand Amudan even better in those times and felt closer to him.

He found answers to some questions that were raging for years in his mind while others fell muted, meaningless now. He felt more at ease with himself, with God, and with his father.

He still couldn't pray but was putting up a solid defence for Amudan before the Lord and his consort with all his might. He found great comfort in his father's words as the latter said to him, "*This is not your Supreme Court to fight for justice. It is the court of the Supreme! We only can sit and watch. The strongest will be put through a test of fire, only to show them in blazing light! Like the great Kings Harishchandra and Nala, for those in selfless pursuits, it becomes the duty of God to protect. We will see Amudan come out of this even stronger!*"

With the beginning of the festivities in the temple, Amudan could hardly hold back his throbbing spirit and his urge to know if everything was in order. He couldn't discuss much, for he didn't know if he was allowed that liberty.

He sat outside the temple next to the old man minding the footwear counter waiting to hear from any of the volunteers walking in and out of the temple. He would yearningly look at each one of them and they would open up to him about the status of the arrangements, and if they needed some guidance.

It wasn't easy for anyone, devotees, *Archakas* or the trustees, even those who were spiting him all along.

Watching Amudan quietly sit coiled in a corner left a gnawing sense of discomfort in them all. For some of them, it was too unbearable!

"You are a King, free to walk where you choose. No one can bind you, Amuda!" said Kumaran's father.

"You will walk into the temple with me. Let me see who will stop you," he challenged.

Watching Amudan stand with his head bowed down, he cupped Amudan's cheeks in his palms and said, "*Raja*, you are our glowing Sun! If you turn gloomy, where will we go? Don't lose heart, Amuda! Who can hide you away? For how long? Your parents and I gave away our two able sons to serve this town, not trusting anyone else but the God resting inside. He will not let us down," he reassured, patting Amudan's cheeks.

Even Ranganayaki's *thinnai* sessions with the ladies of the town were lacklustre these days. She hardly stepped out of the house and even those times, few and far between, was only found sniffling and lamenting," Who is interested in cooking anymore? It's been days since we even sat down to eat one proper meal. How can we? Amudan is like a son to us. I cannot bear to see that child's face this way!"

Perundevi was also in her thoughts. For only a mother can feel the pain of another at watching her child suffer.

Ranganayaki felt lost for words, for once! For her words never could express her emotions as much as they knew to mask them!

While she always prided herself on Komala's achievements and capabilities, no one knew of her secret wish to bear a son. Having watched Amudan through his growing years and in close quarters, little Amudan was indeed the son she wished she had! With the birth of Komala, her joy doubled no doubt, but her affection for Amudan remained.

Though everyone knew how tactfully Ranganayaki could extract work from Amudan, only she knew the number of times she thought about him in a day. Every time she wanted to sulk of the heat or her daily toils in the kitchen, she thought of Amudan slogging it out right under the blazing sun in the fields each day. She instantly fell quiet, having nothing to complain about.

She only made it a point to offer to Amudan at least a morsel of food that she had cooked. Nothing brought her more joy and relief than watching him frown and gulp down a fistful of her *Dhadhyonnam or* the *Thirukannamudu* that she offered in a silver tumbler.

Even when the whole town acclaimed Amudan, touting his almost overnight journey to riches, she tried hard to quell all malign rumours with the narratives she spread. While she quietly worried all along, hoping he wouldn't land in trouble. Now her quiet prayers only grew more fervent!

The arrangements for the temple festivities were all done and the procession of the Lord was to begin in some time. This time without Amudan and Kumaran leading the pack of *Sripadamthangis*.

It was a day-long struggle for Manikandan to come to terms with the situation. He stood by Amudan, keeping him abreast of the status of the preparations and activities all day. Amudan finally, with a peek at his watch, prompted that it was time and signalled for the boy to go into the temple.

"*Anna*, I am not able to do this. I will also stay out of the temple, *Anna,*" pleaded Manikandan.

Amudan, who was seated on a stone next to the temple footwear stand, looked up at Manikandan with disbelief.

Seeing his tear-filled eyes, Amudan placed his palm on Manikandan's feet and said, "Get in, it's time."

Shocked by the gesture and turning chill with emotions, Manikandan wriggled his feet out and leapt into the temple, wiping his eyes off the tears splashing out.

To the awe and admiration of everyone, the trained brigade of volunteers, the *Sripadamthangis*, like soldiers on a mission, ensured that the festivities went on without a hitch keeping up with Amudan's standards, schedule and efficiency.

Amudan was indeed in all their thoughts and prayers now!

Churn

An unresolved puzzle looming over their heads, the *Archakas* among others, holding the first line of responsibility, felt that all their dignity and pride were put at stake. With doubts on each other, and enduring the suspecting glances of a few others, they treaded on a path of fire each day. More careful about what they spoke or did, everyone quietly went about their temple duties, aware of the one man who was suffering for one of them. They were kinder to each other and more humble now.

Govindan never left the side of *Thaayaar,* with tear-laden eyes and a resolve not to speak a word other than the *Archana* he recited for the Goddess or the scriptures he read and only more frugal with what he ate, he immersed himself in spiritual pursuits all day until he wept himself to sleep, in brief spells each night.

Amudan was tired now. It was more than a week. Every pain he knew would heal with time, but strangely, his pain this time was only getting worse with every passing moment. It was draining him.

At every ding of the temple bell, he could never sit still. Restless as a bat volleying between walls, he walked up to the temple entrance and back all day. He sat near the footwear stand outside the temple and watched people walk in and out, eagerly looking into the faces of devotees. Those who walked out triumphantly charged up, stronger and ready to take on their lives.

For him though, his life lay right inside, majestically stretched on a serpent! *Will I get to see his smile just one more time?* He couldn't stop pining. The devotees walking in and out of the temple, whom he had always screened with discerning eyes, he now looked with deep reverence and an aching heart. He sat watching them all day, his eyes glued to the temple entrance.

It was the last day of the festivities and Amudan sat outside waiting for the volunteers to come out after the *Uchikaala Pooja*. Not having the energy to keep his eyes open, he dozed off, leaning on the wall behind him. He couldn't feel the heat, even as he sat right under the blazing sun at noon. Watching him fast asleep, the frail old man at the footwear stand, his hands now shivering more with emotions, slowly moved the canopy covering the slippers over Amudan. Everyone who knew Amudan, even those who despised him all along, had by now dispensed with all their hate. There was only compassion and overwhelming sympathy they could feel for him.

What can be said of the people who truly cared for him? Komala, as she walked out of the temple, found Amudan asleep seated near the slipper stand, meek and fragile as a starved animal. Unable to bear the sight, she sprinted off to her home, dialling Kumaran's number on the way.

Hearing Komala's distressed tone, Kumaran rushed to the spot in a few minutes.

"Amuda! Amuda!" he called out as he shook Amudan awake, throwing an arm around him. Amudan woke up with a blistering headache, holding his temple in his palm. He could hardly open his eyes. He heard Kumaran's voice as the latter pulled him up to his feet and led him to the bike.

"You will not leave this place till I ask you to," yelled Kumaran, dragging Amudan back home. Ramanujam stood, shocked to see Amudan, in the state he was.

"What is your work at the temple? Haven't they thrown you out? Don't you have any shame?" went on Kumaran as Amudan sank to the ground.

Watching Amudan quietly seated with his head hung down, Kumaran asked, "It hurts a lot, doesn't it?" holding Amudan by his shoulders.

"Will you tell me who took the nose ring? You know I will protect anybody if that is what you want. We can find another way out. Please, will you tell me?" beseeched Kumaran. "I can find it out myself, but I am not able to do it against you..." Amudan was shocked to see Kumar.an break into tears.

"Amuda, you know nothing matters to me more than your happiness. Not this town, not this temple or not *Perumal*. I can do anything. I cannot see you like this anymore." He choked with words.

"Not just me. Can you not see all of them suffering?" He asked, pointing towards Perundevi and Ramanujam. "How much longer? It is unbearable, Amuda!" Seeing Amudan stare ahead blankly, Kumaran squatted before him, forcing Amudan to look at him.

"Who is that person you are trying to protect with your life? That one life you consider dearer than all ours?" At that moment, when their eyes met, Kumaran seemed to have found his answer.

Amudan shut his eyes tight, resting his head on the wall behind him.

"No one will question my son about anything in this house," declared Ramanujam.

As Kumaran turned to him, Ramanujam with folded hands gestured for Kumaran to follow him outside the house.

"Kumara, I have skinned him alive when he was a little boy. He has never shed a drop of tears. I have insulted him, tortured him, done all that I can to keep him away from the temple, only I grew tired. I couldn't hold him back even for a minute. Like a whirlwind, he will go rustling all over. I only watched in wonder. I have never seen him rest. We will never know if he was unwell. We would hear him thunder from afar."

"All that has gone in a sweep, Kumara! In one moment! We have not heard his voice for almost a week now. You don't know how he struggles to swallow one scoop of food these days. You don't know what a pain it is to watch him sit and stare at his plate. I don't care what the whole world thinks of him. I don't want to prove anything. Let them call him a thief or a fool. I don't care! I only want one thing from your *Perumal*! To keep my son alive wherever.." He choked and shook with tears.

"Both of you come inside. Amudan is waiting for you to have food," prompted Perundevi. Ramanujam sped in, wiping his face dry, to join Amudan for lunch.

Just as the three men sat to eat, they heard the frail voice of Sowmya say, "*Anna,* can you come home?"

She tore into the house in tears. "He is not well. Something is wrong with him. He is not talking coherently. I am afraid!"

Amudan leapt to his feet and rushed to Govinda's house, with Kumaran following him.

After a sleepless seven nights and a more punishing schedule at the temple, with festival days around, Govindan could hardly get his limbs to move. Shivering and moaning, he lay coiled on the floor with a burning fever.

As Amudan and Kumaran ran into Govindan's house, they saw Narayana *Bhattar* was already there, rubbing Govindan's palm.

"Am I losing my hands? Don't touch my hand, please! It is impure and maligned now. I carried it home in these hands. How could I? I should have put it back." He lamented, as *Bhattar* slowly turned to see Amudan and Kumaran.

"*Amma*, how did I have the heart to take it from you?" he went on "Couldn't you stop me right then?" he entreated the Goddess.

"Govinda! Stop blabbering! Wake up!" yelled Amudan as he stepped closer. His voice was firm and loud.

"Amuda! Amuda! Is it you? It was on my lap, Amuda. I promise I didn't take it, Amuda! Will you forgive me? Will you talk to me again?" Govindan cried aloud, still delirious.

Amudan rushed to his side, lifting Govindan by his shoulders, and held his back in his arms.

"Amuda, have you forgiven me? Tell me you have forgiven me. I have said everything to *Bhattar* Mama. Forgive me, *Da*, it was too heavy. I couldn't hold it any longer. What if I die without getting a chance to speak the truth? "pleaded Govindan, bursting into tears. Amudan held him tight.

"You will be all right, Govinda. Don't be scared. Let's go to the doctor first," said Amudan, patting Govindan's cheek and forcing his eyes open. Govindan, with the innocence of a child, smiled at Amudan.

"Don't take me anywhere! Keep me on your lap. I have told the truth!" He beamed with relief. "I have told that you are blemishless. I am the one to be thrown out. If one of us has to leave, it has to be me, Amuda, not you," he breathed, looking into Amudan's eyes. Amudan, unable to combat Govindan's pleas, vainly covered the latter's mouth with his palm and said to *Bhattar*, "He did not take it. Don't punish him, please!" implored Amudan.

Bhattar shook his head, his eyes welling up.

"You have already punished him. How can someone punish him more?" asked *Bhattar*.

"You have punished all of us," he said with folded hands, remembering the painful moments of the past week watching the young man before him throw away his life and everything he had toiled for in a trice and quietly walk away.

His own actions and words at Amudan shocked him more at every recall. He was not himself then, he could see. He was able to understand Govindan's anguish even better. There is no better punishment for an act than one's repentance.

"Don't worry, Govinda. No one will throw you out! Who am I, anyway?" said *Bhattar* heaving a deep sigh.

"Govinda, you in fact revealed the truth to me the same day the nose ring was found. The same afternoon when you innocently walked up to me with the nose ring saying, "*Can any of you please try to put it on for Thaayaar? Every time I tried, I have only failed. My hands have now become too impure perhaps*," and you burst into tears. I was shocked by your words. While the rest of us tried to put it on *Thaayaar*, we all still failed. "

"That's when I thought this was for sure the act of the divine! I could have pushed you harder. I still kept quiet, knowing how your friend was guarding the truth with his life. How can I let him down? I could never do that," he said, looking into Amudan's tear-smeared eyes.

He could only see a little boy hiding from his father behind the door at the shrine of Lord Amudan, looking with fear at Bhattar, as the latter covered up for him, saying, "*Are you looking for Amudan, Mama? He never came here*!"

Exhausted and overcome with emotions, Govindan swooned and lay in Amudan's arms. Kumaran announced that the ambulance would be there at any moment.

Sowmya, as she was getting ready to leave for the hospital, scooted over to *Bhattar* and handed him a small cloth bundle, saying, "Please take it as our humble contribution to *Thaayaar*. I will never ask to wear any jewel again, ever! I only beg her to bring back my husband to life."

Bhattar, putting the cloth of jewels back into her hands, said, "*Thaayaar* does not care for these jewels as much as she cares for all of you- her children. She had only shown to the world the worth of each one of you. It is a divine play, that is all. She threw one diamond nose ring only to show the real "gems" that she owned, more precious than all the gold and diamonds in the world.

"You will wear all of it and come to the temple with your husband soon," *Bhattar* blessed her heartily.

Amudan and Kumaran went to the hospital with Govindan. Once the fever was arrested, Govindan crept back to normalcy.

A Sunset

Every sunset is special. A beautiful reminder of a day gone by. The inexplicable relief that is felt through those serene, still moments, when even worries and fear seem to take a recess in its breathtaking glow. A balm that heals all the weariness and wounds from a day's toil, a rough journey or gruesome memories of the past. It brings along a fresh scent of hope that even the most unsurmountable challenge will settle as dust soon, someday!

It was indeed one such memorable sunset the town witnessed. People thronged at the temple, as they usually did every Friday evening, to watch the procession of *Thaayaar*, but this time, though, to watch a more momentous sight! As the curtains were drawn open and *Thaayaar*'s palanquin emerged out of it, all their hearts fluttered with joy to watch Amudan and Kumaran in the front on either side bearing the palanquin and the Goddess seated above, her glow and majestic gait. Like a proud mother, flanked by her virtuous sons!

Was it the *Thiruman Sricharanam* and sandalwood tilak they bore on their foreheads, that shone brightly, or was it the shimmering glow of their virtues that were blinding them all? Everyone watched them spellbound, with a sense of personal victory, the relief of holding something very precious, that was lost and found.

As for Amudan's state of mind, all through the past week, being cast away from the only world he has known, the pain it left him with, was hard to imagine!

Amudan, at times, sat observing himself, as he went about his days, carrying what seemed like a heavy lump that kept moving between his chest and throat. He couldn't cough it up or cry it out, nor could he bear the heaviness of it as well. He thought he would succumb anytime. Looking around at his family and friends, the pain in all their eyes, he felt as if they were already mourning his death. He waited to watch how it would end. Would he just stop breathing all of a sudden or would he choke to death? In fact, he wondered as to what kept him alive this long. *That was his only hope,* he thought, *that things would turn for the better soon*!

The next morning as Govindan resumed his duties at the temple, under the compulsion of Vasu *Bhattar,* Govindan tried again to put the nose ring on for *Thaayaar,* with Amudan, Vasu *Bhattar* and Kumaran watching on. With no effort needed, to all their joy and relief, she wore it on finally! Vasu *Bhattar* euphorically ran, announcing to Narayana Bhattar, "*Anna, Thaayaar* accepted the nose ring from Govindan!"

While Amudan, Kumaran, and Govindan, quietly savoured those ecstatic moments in each other's company. A divine play, it was indeed, and watching the three of them smile now, was perhaps Her ultimate triumph!

It was not the end of difficult times for the town though. With a low-pressure building over the Bay of Bengal, there was a warning of very heavy rains in South India.

Heavy rains began to lash across the town. The streets were inundated, many trees uprooted, people immobilised, and some displaced from their flooded homes.

Kumaran, who was out of town on business, was still held up due to the rains.

Amudan was preoccupied with dealing with the crisis, plying people around, and attending to every call for assistance. With Kumaran's bike, his business vans and trucks all available for their use, Amudan and a few other volunteers were all over and on the move, driving a cart, truck, or a van on vigil.

Malli was a month away from her delivery date. With all the nourishment and care, her anaemic condition was largely managed so far. She was praying and hoping the rains would stop soon as her helper hadn't turned up the last few days due to the rains. Knowing the plight of everyone in the town, she didn't feel it was right to inform anyone about it. More than anything, she knew that Amudan was just a call away.

She managed most of her work herself, talking to the little one in her womb for company, and narrating stories from her childhood. She cherished those moments alone with her unborn child. The rest of the time, she was always anxious, and couldn't eat or sleep properly.

It was another dawn, but the rains were still unyielding. With no power supply the whole day, and the wild howl of the winds lashing, the shimmering light from the hurricane lamp was her only strength that night.

All of a sudden, she observed something strange with the movement of the baby in her womb. She panicked.

She dialled Amudan in despair. She was breathing hard even as she kept dialling in vain. She couldn't reach Amudan, Komala, or her neighbour. None of her calls went through.

She slowly stepped out of the house in the middle of the night and cried aloud for help. Alas, in the noise of the thunder and the torrential rain, her frail voice could hardly make it through. She didn't have the energy to stand, walk or even pray.

Amudan woke up with a start from a terrible nightmare. One that he could vividly recall, where the water had flooded right into the temple and all over the shrine of Lord Aravamudan encompassing the magnificent deity lying on the *Adisesha*. The next moment, he could only see a cradle in the shrine with a child lying in it and water rising to the child's neck. He sat dazed and reached for his phone to check the time when he saw messages coming in.

He was in Kumaran's van the next moment, noticing he had several missed calls from Malli.

Malli was cold and shivering, lying outside her house. Amudan, taking the help of a lady in the neighbourhood and her son, rushed Malli to the hospital.

Given her health condition, the doctors advised an emergency caesarean procedure to save the mother and the child. Everything happened in no time. The nurse came out of the labour room all the way to Amudan and showed him a glimpse of the baby born. Amudan craned his neck to look at the baby nestled in the nurse's arms. He involuntarily put his palms together at the precious sight.

She indeed looked like a deity, her face pink and tender as a freshly bloomed lotus.

"We could only save the child," the doctor announced with a sombre expression. Amudan gasped, holding his chest in shock, barely able to hear anything more of what the doctor was saying.

The child was kept under observation and care while discharge formalities were underway. One hospital staff, a volunteer at the temple, was helping Amudan around with the formalities.

As he was handed the bill, Amudan said, "I will have to go and fetch money. I haven't brought anything"

"*Anna*, you stay here. Tell me where I should get the money from," replied the volunteer.

Amudan taking a while to think, removed the gold chain that Bhooma had given him and, handing it over to the volunteer, said, "Can you give this to Chettiar *Mama* and tell him I asked for money?"

The boy fetching Amudan's chain sped out to Chettiar's home.

It was just about dawn. The rains had taken recess after all the wreck it played, leaving behind a quiet and gloomy town. Just outside the hospital, the volunteer halted on seeing Komala and Malli's helper come rushing in, devastated by the news.

When Komala asked him where he was headed, the volunteer showed her the chain and said he was going to fetch money from the Chettiar. Komala, reaching her hand out, took Amudan's chain from the boy, saying, "I have money. Come in."

As they walked into the ward, Komala saw Amudan standing at the entrance of a room. She watched him look anxiously at the volunteer rushing back to him and the palpable relief on his face seeing her come. The volunteer sped to Amudan and informed him of the change of plan, and the latter merely nodded in assent.

The hospital bills were all settled. The newborn was to be under observation and care for a few more days.

Since Malli had no surviving close relatives and her distant relative who lived far away didn't communicate any intention of attending her funeral, the last rites were done under the directions of the elders of the town. Komala and Amudan, grieving with all their hearts. When the question of guarding the child came up, Komala and Amudan volunteered in unison. Narayana Bhattar, stepping in for Komala, said, "Since it's a girl child, we will take care of her in our house until we hear from Malli's relatives."

Amudan left it at that.

This stirred up a storm in Bhattar's house with Ranganayaki blowing the roof over the decision of her husband. She howled and wailed all day, asking, "Did you even realise you have an unmarried daughter at home? How can we raise that newborn in our house? Are there not other "homes" that can take care of "these" children? How will we explain this to the prospective groom families? Can't you see our daughter is immature, how did you have the heart to indulge this wish of hers? " She went on.

With the child being brought home, Ranganayaki's hands got fuller and not finding her on the *Thinnai* these days, the neighbouring ladies would walk into Bhattar's house to meet her. Ranganayaki rambled on about her plight now, her irresponsible husband and her foolish daughter, while never for a moment placing the child down.

Amudan at every opportunity would walk in to steal a glance at the child and if he were lucky, even get to mind her.

When Komala returned his gold chain, Amudan without taking it, replied," *It's hers now,*" faintly smiling at the child.

From then on, Ranganayaki called the child "*Seematti*!" referring to the fortune the little one had already made and never missed an opportunity to tell everyone how blessed the child was. Only she knew how much it hurt every time she heard the child cry!

Komala, though, was initially upset over her mother's disapproval and resistance, but the sight of her mother rushing and getting on her knees at the first feeble cry of the child warmed her heart.

The little one was named "Kodhai"!

Is there a replacement for a mother's love? Even if there were a hundred pairs of hands that could cuddle and comfort a crying child, can that make up for a mother's warmth? She could have been born blind, deaf, dumb, or crippled any other way! She would not have known what she didn't have so long as she had a mother to look out for her. For there is no greater protection for the child than a mother who worries for her night and day, all her life!

Ranganayaki was no different. She was a mother first, and it was sleepless nights for her ever since Kodhai entered their home. As much as she tended to the child with compassion, there was not a moment of respite from her worrying about Komala's future. She seethed with anger at the thought!

She started fervently scouting for a suitable alliance for Komala through all sources. She stopped consulting her husband, or Komala, in these matters.

She at one time said to Narayana Bhattar, "I have lost the trust that you even want to see our daughter married. Remember, you have also lost your say in this matter! My decision will be final!" They sparsely exchanged words since then.

Every time Komala was found in the company of the child, Ranganayaki would have a loud conversation with a neighbour or on the phone about "a good alliance" that had come. The words, "The boy is in the "US"...."Australia"......"Canada" troubled her even more! Komala had to live in constant fear.

Komala didn't wish to speak to anyone about it. If at all, she knew there was only one who could help her. She trusted Lord Aravamudan blindly, beyond her fears!

It was just about a month since Kodhai was born. Out of the blue, Narayana Bhattar had a strange visitor, an aunt of Malli and her husband, from a distant town.

From Ranganayaki's warmth and welcoming tone, it was quite clear that the couple weren't there uninvited, if not under pressure. By dint of her persistence, persuasion, dexterity and force, Ranganayaki had hunted them down and made sure the couple turned up at the earliest to take custody of the child.

Packing off a bag of essentials for the child, with a heart of steel, she handed it to Malli's aunt, saying, " I don't wish to delay your journey. Will you reach your place before dinner? I have also packed some dinner for you." She added warmly.

Narayana Bhattar sat shell-shocked and helplessly watching the events happening before his eyes. " Can you wait till my daughter comes home? " He meekly requested the guests as Ranganayaki cut in saying, "What are you saying? No! No! We cannot hold them up for that long. We will explain to her. They will have to travel with an infant, remember? They better reach home at a decent hour."

Narayana Bhattar was left muted and helpless.

"Where is Kodhai?" Amudan asked, looking around, not finding her in the living room.

Ranganayaki, without lifting her head from her phone, coolly replied," Malli's aunt and Uncle were here. They have taken Kodhai with them. They want to take care of the child. "

"What!! Why? Who are they? Where have they taken her?" he bawled. Ranganayaki shuddered at the tone and rose to her feet as he yelled, "Did you just give away the child?"

Bhattar, who was outside resting on his easy chair, rushed in, hearing Amudan's words. He saw Ranganayaki stand trembling before Amudan.

"Amuda! Don't shout! What do you want to know?" He asked.

"Why did they take Kodhai? Why did you allow them?" He demanded.

"They are Malli's family. Ranganayaki knows them. They were sorry that they couldn't come and see Malli all these years. They wanted to raise her child now. Who are we to stop them? The child should be with her family. It is good for her. It was the only right thing to do in these circumstances," declared Bhattar.

Amudan shook his head in disbelief, and without another word, stormed out of the house. Livid and helpless, he could hardly think. He mindlessly hopped onto his bicycle and sped away. He couldn't believe that they had now lost the child as well, alive! His eyes welled with tears at the thought.

Racing with his thoughts, he rode on at a blinding speed, aimlessly; the wind splashing away the torrent of tears gushing down his cheeks. Malli's pale, pain-stricken eyes, in her last moments of battle, kept flashing in his mind!

After a long battle that night over the phone with Desikan, exploring legal ways by which he could bring Kodhai back to the town, he finally hung up crestfallen, when Desikan said, "You can never adopt her until you get married!"

Surrender

"Why Amma? What was the hurry? We were trying to do everything legal for the protection of the child. Why did you send her away now? You could have spoken to me!" Komala bleated in shock. "Did you consult Desikan?" she asked, turning to her father. He shook his head.

"Does Amudan know?" she breathed, her eyes turning red and damp. *Bhattar* shut his eyes, running his palm over it, Amudan's look of despair still lingering in his mind.

Kodhai indeed took along with her the life of the house. Amudan never came to their house ever since the day she left.

Komala though was herself extremely pained by her mother's action, knew that Amudan would only be more shaken by it. As much as she wanted to talk to him and pour her heart out, she never dared to even look him in the eye.

Finally, one evening as Komala returned from school, Ranganayaki, while handing her a tumbler of coffee, casually said, "You have to take a leave of absence from school tomorrow. A groom's family will be visiting us. "

Komala grew numb at hearing her mother's words. Not that she was shocked. It was a familiar feeling of pain she had felt when Kodhai was moved out of the house.

"For the good of the child," as her mother had stressed every time, trying to justify her action.

"*Naadaatha malar naadi naal thorum naaranan than Vaadaatha malaradikkeezh vaikkave vakukkinru*"

The pasuram of Saint *Nammazhwar*, where the saint sends a cool breeze as a messenger to the Lord saying, "*Was I not born to gather the rarest of flowers and place them at the feet of Lord Narayana every day? Why does he then let me wither, far away from him?*"

Komala, taking refuge in this pasuram, wrote a few lines of a letter, addressed to the Lord Aravamudan, pouring her heart out to him.

She placed it in the middle of the garland she had strung and handed the basket to a volunteer, whom Amudan had sent to fetch the flowers.

As Amudan walked out after placing the garland and flowers on the silver tray at the shrine of Lord Aravamudan, he noticed a small piece of paper stuck to the fold of his *angavastram* tucked to his hip.

He opened it and couldn't resist reading the beautiful handwritten piece.

"There are thousands of flowers
That you carry on your shoulders every day,
Am I not as dear as any of them?
Was I not born to serve you as well?
Why do you want to shunt me away, my Lord?
Am I too much of a burden to bear?
Or have you exhausted all your kindness on me?
Where will I go then, Oh Lord Amuda?
If you cannot spare any more of your sweetness for me!
Pray, do not cast me too far away now!
Not beyond the fortress of your temple walls,
Or the reach of the corner of your compassionate eyes.
This flower cannot survive anywhere else, remember!
Don't let anyone take her away!"

From the strokes and the tenor, he was sure it was Komala's writing.

"*What was she talking about?*" He wondered. "*Who could take her away? Or was it about Kodhai?*"

He was in two minds, whether to put it back in the flower basket or not. He read it again. This time, it left a tug in his heart.

He watched Komala from afar, as she stood outside *Thaayaar Sannidhi* looking at the Goddess inside in rapt attention.

He walked around the *prakaram* immersed in thoughts. The *kolams* she had just drawn were all around, decorating the temple passage. He wished he could inscribe each one of them for posterity. He couldn't imagine the temple floors without them. Sure, there would be hundreds of others who would clamour to fill in. *Can we find another Komala among them?*

As he approached the entrance of Lord Aravamudan, he could hear Vasu Bhattar talking in a hush to the Madapalli swami.

"It's a first-class alliance, *Swamin*! The boy is an engineer settled in the US, it seems. Perfect match for Komala. Call it providence or *Mami*'s prudence! Soon *Bhattar Anna* will also migrate to the US, mark my words," he quipped.

The words fell like thunder on Amudan. He tiptoed into the shrine. Narayana *Bhattar* was busy as always. Being a crowded day, he barely made eye contact with the devotees and was focused on the *Archana* he was doing.

Finally, when the *Aarthi* was shown to Lord *Aravamudan*, Bhattar, in his majestic voice, recited the *pasuram* of *Thirumazhisai Azhwar* on Lord *Aravamudan*

"Nadantha kaalgal nondhavo Nadunghu jnala menamaay
Idanthamey kulunghavo vilanghu maal varaicchuram
kadandhakaal parandha kaavirikkarai kudanthaiyul
Kidanthavaar ezhundhirundhu pesu vaazhi kesane!"

Where the *Azhwar* awakens, the Lord reclined on the celestial serpent at Thirukudanthai on the banks of river Cauvery, saying,

"*Are your legs hurting after walking in search of Mother Sita? Oh, Kesava! Please, will you rise and speak to me?*"

People who frequented the temple or those who had visited before were familiar with Narayana Bhattar's distinct way of serving the Lord and presenting to the devotees an exalted spiritual experience with the sheer divinity in his manners and tone, especially as he recited this pasuram while performing the *Aarti*. Devotees would be left overwhelmed, some crying along, "*Govinda! Govinda*!" at the end of the *pasuram*.

Today it was on a different plain though, when Bhattar, choking with emotions, barely could utter the last few words of the *pasuram,* his voice shaking and tears raining down from his eyes, his hands trembling as he held the *Aarti* before the Lord. Devotees indeed stood enthralled. Amudan, unable to bear the sight, quietly slipped out of the shrine unnoticed.

Ranganayaki, though, was unyielding! Early the next evening, well before the temple opening time, Amudan and Manikandan were seated outside the temple, looking into the budget for the annual temple festival.

Two cars entered the temple street and came to a halt before *Bhattar*'s house. Amudan watched a group of men and women being warmly welcomed by Ranganayaki and Narayana *Bhattar*.

Amudan tried hard to concentrate on the job in his hand. In a short while, when Amudan was on a call, he heard loud shrieks and squeals from *Bhattar*'s house. Amudan and Manikandan rushed to the house when he heard Bhattar's voice saying, "Call Amudan!"

"A snake! Inside!" stuttered Ranganayaki on seeing Amudan at the entrance. He quietly walked in.

A serpent lay right on the entrance step to Komala's room. He saw her, bejewelled and decked up in a silk saree, calmly seated, her eyes fixed on the snake spread right before her. She slowly looked up at him. What a relief it was to see Amudan at that moment!

Amudan looked around and picked up a sack from a corner. He valiantly lifted the tail end of the snake, holding the sack open on the other end. As the snake swiftly charged into the sack, he gripped the sack close and coolly walked away like he was holding a bunch of spinach in hand.

With a passing glance at a young man coiled up on a chair, seated on all fours, Amudan's eyes lit up with a smile. It was the groom who was the first to rush to the car just minutes later!

The snake and Komala were thus rescued in time!

A few days later, Amudan was at the shrine of Lord Aravamudan, minding the place at *Bhattar*'s request, while the latter was away on some personal commitment. Savouring the precious moments of the private audience he could have with the Lord, Amudan picked up the huge hand fan and began to fan the Lord reclined before him.

"*Amma*, please do not force me into this. I will not be happy at all," he heard Komala's voice approaching close.

Bhattar stormed into the shrine, followed by his wife and daughter.

"Listen to me, Komala. I will never do anything that will be detrimental to you. Trust me. The boy is very well educated and has settled well in a job in the US. I know the family so well. I want you to have a comfortable life, Komala. He has already bought one house for his parents in India and another in the US."

"Amma, what are you talking about!" Komala hissed.

"Quiet, both of you. We are here before the Lord. We will seek his approval on this. Will you both agree to abide by his word?" He asked, looking at Ranganayaki and Komala.

"Perumal has already indicated his disapproval, isn't it?" Komala whined, "Where did the snake come from? They didn't even get to see me. What more sign of disapproval can you have?"

"Stop that, Komala. You will do as we say. Stop talking! Let Appa seek Perumal's word on it. I will abide by it," declared Ranganayaki.

"I will also go with the word of the Lord undoubtedly. But *Amma* is not going to stop with this. She will bring another alliance- a boy from another continent. I don't know how I can make you all understand. I cannot do this, *Appa*. Please spare me the drill.

I don't wish to leave this town at all. Please don't send me away, *Appa*. I beg!" she said, crying like a child.

Amudan's heart cuddled at the sight.

"Don't cry, Komala!" He blurted.

"What do you fear? No one can take you away, don't you worry!" He added.

"Komala, you have a choice. You can either choose to marry this groom who can give you all that your *Amma* wants you to have. There is another guy who has nothing of that, not even a respectable qualification or a job. He can afford nothing much beyond food, shelter and clothing. Just a plain, empty-headed ruffian, with no virtue to his credit! But he can promise you one thing. Only one thing. That he will not let even your shadow fall outside of this town, come what may! "

"Komala, can you marry him? The choice is yours!" He said as he placed the hand fan back in its place.

Smiling through a torrent of tears gushing out of her eyes, Komala looked at her father yearningly.

"*Yaaru da*?" asked Ranganayaki confounded.

"Amudan!" uttered Amudan, patting his chest with pride.

When the garland of *Tulasi* drifted from Lord Aravamudan's neck and fell to the ground.

Bhattar let out a loud hoot of joy crying, "*Narayana! Narayana!* "

Komala, in a fit of emotion, forced her hand out of her mother's hold and stood with hands folded together, staring at the Lord in amazement.

A moment of reckoning indeed, when His grace manifests for all to see, reposing the faith of this child, that every conversation, she has had with Him all these years, was heard and even her most bosom wish, unravelled from deep within, was acknowledged, approved and indeed quietly being blessed. Her path, her future, was now laid right before her like it was handed in a platter for her to choose from!

Ranganayaki slowly turned to see her daughter, whose face was glowing in ecstasy, the tears of joy drenching her cheeks and neck. Ranganayaki heaved a deep sigh of relief.

"Aravamudan"

The story behind the Lord of *Thirukudanthai* goes back to the day when Sage *Bhrigu*, set out on a mission to find out the Supreme of the Gods. When the Sage reached the celestial abode of Lord Vishnu, he saw him reclined on the *Adisesha,* the thousand-headed serpent and Mahalakshmi serving at his feet. Watching the Lord rest blissfully without taking notice of the Sage's arrival there, the Sage kicked the Lord on his chest. Lord Vishnu, who rose immediately, got down from the celestial serpent, and held the feet of the Sage asking, "*Did your tender feet hurt*?" Indeed, Lord Vishnu was declared Supreme, on account of his unparalleled virtues! While Goddess Mahalakshmi was left immensely pained and angered by the incident.

Sage Bhrigu, in deep repentance of his action that had angered Goddess Mahalakshmi, performed rigorous penance in his next birth as Sage *Hemarishi,* to attain Goddess Mahalakshmi as his daughter and give her back in marriage to Lord Vishnu.

It was Lord Vishnu who, heeding to the penance of Sage *Hemarishi* descended in his celestial Chariot as Lord *Aravamudan* in *Thirukudanthai* to take the Sage's daughter Goddess *Komalavalli*'s hand in marriage.

Little Amudan had heard this story many times through his growing years. In all these years of his obsession and devotion to Lord Aravamudan, perhaps it was this virtue of the Lord that he had naturally imbibed! Whatever pain or insult caused by people around him, Amudan would never take it to heart. He only always regretted being a discomfort to them all.

Barring the time when he was ousted from the temple and unable to quell his aching heart, he kept thinking, *"Why haven't I perished yet, now that even Perumal has kicked me out?"*

There was not a speck of resentment in that thought. Nor could he pray, asking to be helped, to be saved or forgiven. He just lay where he was strewn, unquestioningly. In acceptance, in absolute surrender! His life, though, rested on a single spark of hope that he may be called back into the temple anytime. Every nerve and limb in him were ticking for that moment!

How would you describe his passion, his blind devotion, to the one and only purpose of his life? A purpose he had fought the whole world for! It was a mere fascination of a child, looking at the magnificent form of Lord Aravamudan, with all the love a tender heart could hold!

Little did the child know that he had since rested his heart, his faith, and his whole being in the refuge of the ONE whom all sages and scriptures hail as the ultimate haven, and even the realisation of which amounts to the attainment of supreme wisdom. The pinnacle of the purpose of a human born! What started as a blind obsession over that divine form grew within him into an undying flame - a passion beyond himself!

The unquenchable rush of divine energy that it sparked, never let him sit still even one moment. Not in prayer, not in penance, not in quest of any spiritual wisdom!

He plunged himself into service where it was needed, in the paddy fields, the temple, the cowshed and every street or house in the town with no distinction whatsoever and nothing to ask for in return.

He built homes, made families thrive. He gave his all to protect each one of them, yet he remained a child forever lost in love and fascination for that one mighty form that ruled his heart! He was rebuked, laughed at, and even loathed by many, but he remained their guard on duty, formidable and firm. They watched him rise tall and way above them all.

For those that worry and strive for themselves, every step is an effort and their rewards are limited to their choices and strength. While for those who engage in selfless pursuits, life is a journey of infinite blessings! There is no limit to what they can do or endure!

With a gentle protective arm around him in one form or the other, Amudan had indeed come a long way now!

With the wedding dates drawing closer, Ramanujam and Perundevi were having sleepless nights. It was indeed the happiest moment they were looking forward to all their lives. The sheer speed at which Amudan's life was moving with all its highs and lows left them overwhelmed most of the time. Ramanujam could no longer utter the name of his son without choking on the word.

Perundevi's mind went wild with worry, imagining every situation. "*Would she know that she will be living with a man who cares the least about himself? He would never wait for a second serving of food! Would he be able to tend to all her emotional needs? Would she be able to forgive him enough, love him irrespective?"*

With more and more questions hounding her, Perundevi would stand staring at Komala whenever they ran into each other. Smiling through her worry-tainted eyes, she would barely have anything to say.

It was Padma and Bhooma who gave her courage.

"Don't overthink, *Amma*. This is indeed a divine grace. If not a teacher's curse! After having evaded teachers all those years, who thought he would end up this way?" quipped Padma. "Komala is a very smart girl. She will manage him better than any of us, don't worry!" she pacified her mother.

Bhooma, though, was the happiest of the lot. She still couldn't believe her most favourite people were getting married to each other. She hadn't even dreamt of them together and now she could hardly sleep through the fact! With her final semester exams around the corner, she tried hard to stay focused.

Ramanujam's house finally had a makeover to welcome a new member into the family! With Padma and Bhooma arriving a week earlier, a jubilant spirit finally caught on. Between their incessant chatter, squabbles and giggles, they still had the last-minute errands, inviting and other preparations to finish, while grabbing every chance to meet Komala on the way. All their eyes were full of dreams!

And all of a sudden, the big day was here!

With the blessings of *Thaayaar and Perumal,* the wedding rituals commenced early in the morning.

Narayana Bhattar and Ranganayaki stood at the entrance of the wedding hall, extending their warm welcome to the groom's family and the guests.

People from all walks of life- temple priests, Vedic scholars, teachers, school children, farmers, bankers, shopkeepers, business owners and labourers came in grooves. Not to mention Amudan's friends and their families who flew down from different parts of the world.

There were only a few hundred invitations printed, but the unending stream of well-wishers of Amudan and Komala walking in was an overwhelming sight. Ranganathan and Desikan, taking turns between the rituals, the dining hall and the kitchen, Kumaran managing the crowd, greeting and introducing the guests, were on their toes throughout!

Komala decked up in a bright pink silk saree, and adorning the traditional *Andal kondai*, with her jewels and bangles jingle to the resounding "*getti melam*" and the *Nadaswaram*, she finally landed a garland on Amudan's neck.

The sight of Amudan and Komala walking into the Mandapam, holding hands, stole every one of their hearts. Each one in the crowd stood frozen in awe and exhilaration at those moments as they watched the two of them walk arm-in-arm!

Perundevi and Ranganayaki stood dazed by the sheer glow of the sight, watching Amudan and Komala emerge as one before their eyes!

Their whole lives, all their toil, seemed to have found their purpose in just that moment. Their eyes fell on each other almost involuntarily. They could neither hold their tears nor their smiles. They blessed their children with all their hearts.

As Amudan knotted the "*Thirumangalyam*" around Komala's neck, and applied the *kumkuma* on her forehead, he watched her quiver like a flower with folded hands, perched on her father's lap. He melted at the sight.

He was reminded of the words from her letter that read, "*Am I not a flower as dear as them?*" He felt a surge of emotions, of compassion, reverence and love his heart could hardly hold! Through the unending shower of flowers on them and amidst the loud cheers and frenzy around, Komala felt his soft dewy eyes delve into hers. She shuddered and gasped, tears of exultation brimming her eyes!

Govindan carrying the garlands and *prasadams* brought along blessings from *Thaayaar and Perumal* for the newlywed. Sowmya, pregnant with their first child, stood beside her husband, radiant and replete as a full moon!

That night, Amudan was still taking stock of the changes made to the room, the dim lights and the dark curtains and more amused to find some of his old sketches neatly framed and hung on the wall. He heard a knock at the door and turned.

He froze as he watched Komala walk in clad in a copper sulphate blue-coloured silk saree.

The same saree he vividly remembered from his dream a few years back and recalled the incident thereafter. He dropped his head immediately at the thought until something dark moving beneath the saree caught his attention. He forged ahead and instinctively lifted her saree, almost squatting at her feet! She squealed out of fear, beating his hand down. It was her darkened *mehendi*-painted toes, not the rat again! They, though, had a lot to talk and laugh about that night.

Amudan and Komala's wedding was common folklore for a very long time, the daily glimpse of the young couple soothing all their eyes and hearts. Their wedding set the vibe for many more auspicious occasions to come. Kumaran consented to marry his cousin, for one!

Much to their joy and relief, Amudan and Komala, in a few months, brought home little Kodhai, as their daughter, in due compliance with all the legal formalities for the adoption of the child.

Govindan and Sowmya delivered a baby boy. They named him "*Aravamudan!*"

GLOSSARY

Aaravamude Adiyen (Tamil)- A Tamil hymn composed by Saint Nammazhwar.

Aarthi/ Mangala Aarthi (Sanskrit)- a Hindu ritual where camphor or oil lamp is offered to the deities.

Acharyan (Sanskrit)- Preceptor who imparts wisdom/ dispels ignorance.

Adisesha (Sanskrit)- A celestial serpent.

Agraharam (Sanskrit)- A brahmin neighbourhood in a temple town.

Akka (Tamil)- Sister and also used to reverentially address a senior female person.

Amma (Tamil)- Mother.

Andal kondai (Tamil)- A traditional South Indian hairstyle.

Angavasthram (Sanskrit)- The stole worn by Brahmin men.

Anna (Tamil)- Brother and also used to reverentially address a senior male person.

Appa (Tamil)- Father.

Aradanai (Sanskrit)- The rituals for worship of a Hindu deity.

Athimber (Tamil)- Sister's husband.

Azhwars (Tamil)- The venerated Tamil poet-saints devoted to Lord Vishnu.

Bhattar/Archakar (Sanskrit)- A priest in a Vishnu Temple.

Bonda (Tamil)- A south Indian snack preparation.

Chakarapongal (Tamil)- A popular South Indian dessert.

Chithirai (Tamil)- The Tamil month spanning from mid-April to mid-May.

Da (Tamil)- a friendly way of addressing a male person.

Darshan (Sanskrit)- The beholding of a deity.

Dhadhyonnam (Tamil)- Curd rice served in South Indian Vishnu Temples.
Dharma (Sanskrit)- Code of living as enunciated in Hindu Scriptures.
Dosa Tawa (Tamil)- a griddle used to make Dosa- a South Indian savoury crepe.
Elai vadam (Tamil)- A steamed papad preparation.
Ekadesi (Sanskrit)- The 11th day of lunar cycle in a Vedic calendar month.
Enna (Tamil)- What?
Garudan/ Garuda Azhwar (Sanskrit)- The Vedic deity who is the mount(vehicle) of Lord Vishnu.
Getti melam (Tamil)- The loud beats played on a percussion instrument to mark a significant event in a traditional South Indian wedding.
Goddess Andal (Tamil)- One of the venerated Azhwars and the consort of Lord Ranganatha.
Goddess Mahalakshmi (Sanskrit)- the consort of Lord Vishnu.
Goshala (Sanskrit)- A cowshed.
Goshti (Sanskrit)- An assembly of persons for a common purpose.
Govinda! Narayana! (Sanskrit)- utterance of the names of Lord Vishnu.
Hecharika (Sanskrit)- A caution/ command to rise.
Jangiri (Tamil)- A South Indian dessert preparation.
Kancheepuram (Tamil)- A district in South India.
King Yudhishtra - Eldest of the Five sons of King Pandu in Mahabharata.
Kolam (Tamil)- A traditional drawing on the floor at the entrance.
Ksheerannam (Tamil)- A South Indian preparation made of rice and milk.

Kudanthai (Tamil)- A city in South India now known as Kumbakonam.
Kumbakonam (Tamil)- A city in South India.
Kumkuma (Sanskrit)- Red turmeric powder.
Ma (Tamil)- A reverential/polite manner of addressing a woman/girl.
Madapalli (Tamil)- A kitchen in the temple.
Madhu, Kaitabha (Sanskrit)- Demons referred to in Hindu Scriptures.
Mahabharata - The Indian Epic written by Saint Veda Vyasa.
Mama (Tamil)- An uncle and also used to reverentially address a senior male person.
Mami (Tamil)- An aunt and also used to reverentially address a senior female person.
Mandagapadi (Tamil)- The custom of offering respects to the deities during procession and temple festivals.
Mandapam (Sanskrit)- A pillared hall in the temple.
Manjal (Tamil)- Turmeric.
Mantharai (Tamil)- Leaves of Bauhinia Variegata tree from Tamil Nadu commonly known as Orchid tree.
Marudhani (Tamil)- A paste of Mehendi/ henna leaves, used to draw traditional designs on the palms and feet of Indian women.
Naadaatha malar naadi (Tamil)- A Tamil hymn composed by Saint Nammazhwar.
Nadantha kaalgal (Tamil)- A Tamil hymn composed by Saint Thirumazhisai Azhwar.
Nadaswaram (Sanskrit)- A double reed wind instrument from South India.
Nammazhwar, Thirumazhisai Azhwar, Thirumangai Azhwar (Tamil)- among the 12 venerated Tamil poet-saints devoted to Lord Vishnu.

Nandavanam (Sanskrit)- A garden in the temple.

Navarathri Mandapam (Sanskrit)- A pillared hall in the temple where rituals and festivities take place.

Paah (Tamil)-A expression of pain.

Paalkaara (Tamil)- Milkman.

Pallu – Loose end of a Saree

Parayanam (Tamil)- The ritual of reading Hindu scriptures.

Pasuram (Tamil)- A Tamil hymn composed by the Azhwars.

Perumal (Tamil)- Lord Vishnu, here refers to Lord Aravamudan/ Lord Sarangapani.

Po (Tamil)- Go!

Ponni / Cauvery- (Tamil)- a river in South India.

Porum (Tamil)- Enough!

Prabhandha Goshti (Sanskrit)- a group of men reciting the works of the Azhwars.

Pradakshina (Sanskrit)- The clockwise circumambulation of deities.

Prakaram (Sanskrit)- Outer passage around the sanctum sanctorum.

Prasadam/Thaayaar prasadam (Sanskrit)- Offerings to God shared/distributed to the devotees.

Puliyodare (Tamil)- A tamarind rice speciality served in South Indian Vishnu Temples.

Purnakumbam (Sanskrit)- A traditional custom of offering a pitcher full of water with coconut and mango leaves to invoke divine blessings.

Purushasuktham (Sanskrit)- A hymn from the Vedas.

Rajasik (Sanskrit)- Showing aggressive tendencies.

Sage Bhrigu/ Hemarishi (Sanskrit)- A revered Vedic Sage of Hinduism.

Sahasranama Archana (Sanskrit)- A ritual of worshipping a Hindu deity, by offering flowers along with the chant of 1000 names of the deity.

Salagramam (Sanskrit)- A divine form of Lord Vishnu.

Saree A traditional Indian garment.

Sayana Aarthi (Sanskrit)- The final Aarthi of the day in a temple

Shatari (Sanskrit)- A crown representing the feet of Lord Vishnu.

Sita Kalyana (Sanskrit)- The marriage of Goddess Sita and Lord Rama.

Sloka (Sanskrit)- Sanskrit devotional verses.

Sri Vaishnava sampradaya (Sanskrit)- The tradition and philosophy propounded by Saint Ramanuja.

Srimad Ramayana (Sanskrit)- The Indian epic written by Sage Valmiki.

Sripadamthangis (Tamil)- The bearers of the deities on palanquins/mounts in Vishnu Temples.

Sthapathi (Sanskrit)- A sculptor.

Sudarshana Ashtakam (Sanskrit)- A Sanskrit composition of Saint Vedanta Desika in praise of Lord Sudarshana, the disc, the prominent weapon of Lord Vishnu.

Sungadi – A traditional textile design native to Madurai in South India.

Suprabhatha pooja (Sanskrit)- The first ritual of the day in a temple.

Swamin (Tamil)- Reverential way of addressing a male person.

Tamizh Vedam/ Naalaayira Divya Prabhandam (Tamil)- Tamil hymns sung by the venerated Tamil poet-saints in praise of Lord Vishnu.

Thaayaar (Tamil)- Goddess Mahalakshmi, here refers to Goddess Komalavalli.

Thaayaar Sannidhi (Tamil/Sanskrit)- The shrine of Goddess Komalavalli (Mahalakshmi).
Thatha (Tamil)- Grandfather.
Theertham/ Theertha (Sanskrit)- The holy water served to devotees in temple.
Thinnai (Tamil)- A raised porch at the entrance of a traditional South Indian home.
Thirukannamudu (Tamil)- A South Indian dessert made of milk.
Thirukudanthai (Tamil)- A Vishnu temple/ place in South India.
Thiruman Sricharanam (Sanskrit)- A holy mark worn by men of Sri Vaishnava Sampradaya.
Thirumangalyam (Sanskrit)- The sacred thread knotted around the bride's neck in a traditional Hindu wedding.
Thirumanjanam (Sanskrit)- The ceremonial shower of the deities.
Thirupalli ezhuchi (Tamil)- A Tamil hymn composed by Saint Thondaradi Podi Azhwar.
Tirupanandal (Tamil)- A town in South India.
Tulasi (Sanskrit)- The Holy basil leaves.
Uchikaala pooja (Sanskrit)- The rituals conducted in a temple at Noon.
Ummachi (Tamil)- A colloquial reference of children to God.
Vaa (Tamil)- Come!
Vahana (Sanskrit)- the mounts (vehicles) of the temple deity.
Vahana mandapam (Sanskrit)-The hall where the palanquins/ mounts (vehicles) of the festival deities are kept in a temple.
Veda Parayana Goshti (Sanskrit)- a group of men reciting the Vedas.

Ven Pongal/Pongal (Tamil)- A South Indian preparation made of rice and lentils.
Yaaru (Tamil)- Who?

ABOUT THE AUTHOR

The author is a Chartered Accountant based in Chennai. Raised in a traditional South Indian family, her initiation into Hindu scriptures started from an early age, listening to the discourses of her Guru. This seeded a spiritual bent that grew with age into a deep-rooted fascination for the timeless tenets and the ways of life promulgated in the scriptures and their universal appeal. An avid reader of English classics and novels, a habit that fostered in her an admiration for the language and a penchant for penning her thoughts. The author brought out her first book, *A Ride with the River Man (2020)*, followed by her second book and the sequel to the first one, *The Secret Trove (2021)*.

www.ingramcontent.com/pod-product-compliance
Ingram Content Group UK Ltd.
Pitfield, Milton Keynes, MK11 3LW, UK
UKHW041637190726
13854UKWH00006B/2544

9 798891 867154